THE BRIGHTON BOYS WITH
THE FLYING CORPS

BY

JAMES R. DRISCOLL

The Brighton Boys With The Flying Corps

CHAPTER I

THE BRIGHTON FLYING SQUADRON

"The war will be won in the air."

The headlines in big black type stared at Jimmy Hill as he stood beside the breakfast table and looked down at the morning paper, which lay awaiting his father's coming.

The boys of the Brighton Academy, among whom Jimmy was an acknowledged leader, had been keenly interested in the war long before the United States joined hands with the Allies in the struggle to save small nations from powerful large ones—-the fight to ensure freedom and liberty for all the people of the earth.

A dark, lithe, serious young French lad, Louis Deschamps, whose mother had brought him from France to America in 1914, and whose father was a colonel of French Zouaves in the fighting line on the Western Front, was a student at the Academy. Interest in him ran high and with it ran as deep an interest in the ebbing and flowing fortunes of France. The few letters Mrs. Deschamps received from Louis' soldier father had been retailed by the proud boy to his fellows in the school until they knew them by heart.

Bob Haines' father, too, had helped fan the war-fire in the hearts of the boys. Bob was a real favorite with every one. He captained the baseball team, and could pitch an incurve and a swift drop ball that made him a demi-god to those who had vainly tried to hit his twisters. Bob's father was a United States Senator, who, after the sinking of the Liusitania, was all for war with Germany. America, in his eyes, was mad to let time run on until she should be dragged into the world-conflict without spending every effort in a national getting-ready for the inevitable day. Senator Haines' speeches were matter-of-fact——just plain hammering of plain truths in plain English. Many of his utterances in the Senate were quoted in the local papers, and Bob's schoolmates read them with enthusiasm when they were not too long.

Then, too, a number of the Brighton boys had already entered the service of Uncle Sam. Several were already at the front and had written thrilling letters of their experiences in the trenches, at close grip with the Boches. Still more thrilling accounts had come from some of their former classmates who were in the American submarine service. Other Brighton boys who had gone out from their alma mater to fight the good fight for democracy had helped to fan the flame of patriotism.

So the school gradually became filled with thoughts of war, and almost every boy from fourteen years of age upward planned in his heart of hearts to one day get into the fray in some manner if some longed-for opportunity ever presented itself.

Jimmy Hill—-who was fortunate in that his home was within walking distance of the Academy—-commenced his breakfast in silence. Mr. Hill read his paper and Mrs. Hill read her letters as they proceeded leisurely with the morning meal. The porridge and cream and then two eggs and a good-sized piece of ham disappeared before Jimmy's appetite was appeased, for he was a growing boy, who played hard when he was not hard at some task. Jimmy was not large for his age, and his rather slight figure disguised a wiriness that an antagonist of his size would have found extraordinary. His hair was red and his face showed a mass of freckles winter and summer. Jimmy was a bright, quick boy, always well up in his studies and popular with his teachers. At home Jimmy's parents thought him quite a normal boy, with an unusually large fund of questions ever at the back of his nimble tongue.

Breakfast went slowly for Jimmy that morning when once he had finished and sat waiting for his parents. Mr. Hill was scanning the back page of the paper in deep concentration. Again the big black letters stared out at Jimmy. "The war will be won in the air." Jimmy knew well enough what that meant, or at least he had a very fair idea of its meaning. But he had sat still and quiet for a long time, it seemed to him. Finally his patience snapped.

"Father," he queried, "how will the war be won in the air?"

"It won't," was his father's abrupt reply. Silence again reigned, and Mrs. Hill glanced at her boy and smiled. Encouraged, Jimmy returned to the charge.

"Then why does the paper say it will?"

"For want of something else to say," replied Mr. Hill. "The airships and flying machines will play their part, of course, and it will be a big part, too. The real winning of the war must be done on the ground, however, after all. One thing this war has shown very clearly. No one arm is all-powerful or all necessary in itself alone. Every branch of the service of war must co-operate with another, if not with all the others. It is a regular business, this war game. I have read enough to see that. It is team-work that counts most in the big movements, and I expect that it is team-work that counts most all the way through, in the detailed work as well."

Team-work! That had a familiar ring to Jimmy. Team-work was what the football coach had forever pumped into his young pupils. Team-work! Yes, Jimmy knew what that meant.

"I can give you a bit of news, Jimmy," added Mr. Hill. "If you are so interested in the war in the air you will be glad to hear that the old Frisbie place a few miles out west of the town is to be turned into an airdrome—-a place where the flying men are to be taught to fly. I expect before the war is over we will be so accustomed to seeing aircraft above us that we will not take the trouble to look upward to see one when it passes."

Jimmy's heart gave a great leap, and then seemed to stand still. Only once, at the State Fair, had he seen a man fly. It had so touched his imagination that the boy had scoured the papers and books in the public library ever since for something fresh to read on the subject of aviation. As a result Jimmy had quite a workable knowledge of what an aeroplane really was and the sort of work the flying men were called upon to do at the front.

The Brighton boys were all keen on flying. What boys are not? Their interest had been stimulated particularly, however, by the news, the year before, that Harry Corwin's big brother Will, an old Brighton boy of years past, had gone to France with the American flying squadron attached to the French Army in the field. True, Will was only a novice and the latest news of him from France told that he had not as yet actually flown a machine over the German lines, but he was a tangible something in which the interest of the schoolboys could center.

An airdrome near the town! What wonders would be worked under his very eyes, thought Jimmy. Flying was a thing that no one could hide behind a tall fence. Besides, there were no high fences around the Frisbie place. Well Jimmy knew it. Its broad acres and wide open spaces were well known to every boy at Brighton Academy, for within its boundaries was the finest hill for coasting that could be found for miles. In winter-time, when the hillsides were deep with snow, Frisbie's slope saw some of the merriest coasting parties that ever felt the exhilaration of the sudden dash downward as the bright runners skimmed the hard, frosty surface. The long, level expanse of meadow that had to be crossed before the hill was reached from the Frisbie mansion would be an ideal place for an airdrome. Even Jimmy knew enough about airdromes to recognize that. He waited a moment at the table to take in fully the momentous fact that their own little town was to be a center of activity with regard to aviation.

Then he dashed out to spread the news among his schoolfellows. His particular chums were, like himself, boys whose homes were in the town. Shut out from the dormitory life, they had grouped themselves together, in no spirit of exclusiveness, but merely as good fellows who, although they appreciated the love and kindness of the home folks, yet felt that they wanted to have as much of the spirit of dear old Brighton outside the Academy as inside.

Jimmy caught sight of Archie Fox—-another of the out-boarding squad of Brighton boys, and a special friend of Jimmy's—-hurrying to the Academy.

"Great news for you, Arch!" shouted Jimmy as he joined his chum.

"Shoot!" directed Archie.

And Jimmy told the great news to the astonished and delighted boy.

"Gosh whillikens!" yelled Archie. "A real live hangar in staid old Brighton! Can you beat it? My vote says the 'buddies' should get together and become fliers. Eh, what? The Brighton Escadrille! Oh, boy!"

Further down the street Dicky Mann and Joe Little, both in Jimmy's class at the Academy, and then Henry Benson, known to all and sundry as "Fat" Benson from his unusual size, joined the boys and heard for the first time the stirring news.

It was truly an exciting morning at the Academy. The tidings of great things in store at no far distant future spread like wildfire. Of all the boys, only two of those who lived in the town, Jimmy Hill and Bob Haines, had heard of the project, and none of the regular boarders at the school had heard the slightest suggestion of it. Bob Haines lived with his uncle in the largest residence in the town. What Bob's uncle did not know of what was going on was little. Beside, Bob was the envied recipient of a letter now and again from his father, the senator, which frequently contained some real news of prospective happenings.

Bob held forth at length that memorable morning, and at noon time was still the center of an admiring group, who listened to his comments on all subjects with great respect and invariable attention. Bob was tall and well built; taller than any of the rest of his fellows except two or three. He had a way of standing with his head thrown back and his shoulders squared as he talked which gave him a commanding air. Few boys in the school ever thought of questioning his statements. But that day Bob was so carried away with his subject that he strayed from familiar ground.

"What sort of fellows are they going to train to fly?" asked Joe Little, a shy boy who rarely contributed to the conversation. Joe's mother was a widow who had lived but few years in the town, having moved there to give her only boy such education as he could obtain before her small income was exhausted. Joe was never loud or boisterous, and while he took his part in games and sports, he was ever the first one to start for his home. Being alone with his mother to such an extent, for they lived by themselves in a little cottage near the Academy grounds, Joe had aged beyond his boy friends in many ways. No sign did he ever show, however, of self-assertiveness. His part in discussions was seldom great, and usually consisted of a well-placed query that voiced what each boy present had thought of asking, but had been a moment too late.

Now Bob had no very clear idea just where the new flying material was to come from. A habit of rarely showing himself at a loss for an answer prompted him to reply: "From the men in the army."

"You're wrong, Bob," said Jimmy Hill. "Most of the flying men that will see actual service at the front will be boys like us. I have read a dozen times that it is a boy's game—-flying. Most of us are almost old enough. One article I read said that lots of boys of seventeen got into the flying corps in England. One writer said that he thought the fellows from eighteen to twenty were much the best fliers. If that is so, and it takes some time to train fliers, some of us might be flying in France before the end of the war."

Bob was frankly skeptical. "I see you flying, Jimmy!" was his comment.

"You will have to grow some first.

"Wrong again," said Jimmy in all seriousness. "It's those of us that don't weigh a ton that are going to be the best sort for the flying business, and don't you forget it."

"Jimmy knows a lot about flying," volunteered Archie Fox. "He bones it up all the time."

"I don't pretend to know much about it, but I am going to know more before that airdrome gets started," said Jimmy.

"That's right," said Joe Little quietly. "It won't hurt any of us to get a bit wiser as to what an aeroplane really is nowadays. Where do you get the stuff to read, Jimmy?"

"Everywhere I can," answered Jimmy. "The weeklies and monthlies generally contain something on flying."

"My father can get us some good stuff," suggested Dicky Mann. Mr. Mann, senior, was the proprietor of the biggest store in the town; and while he did not exactly pretend to be a universal provider, he could produce most commodities if asked to do so. The store had a fairly extensive book and magazine department, so Dicky's offer to enlist the sympathies of his father promised to be of real use.

"I'll write to my brother Bill and get him to fire something over to us from France," said Harry Corwin. "There is no telling but what he can put us on to some wrinkles that the people who write things for the papers would never hear about."

"My aunt just wrote me a letter asking me what sort of a book I wanted for my birthday," put in Fat Benson. "I will write to-day and tell her I want a book that will teach me to fly."

This raised a storm of laughter, for Henry Benson's stout figure bid fair to develop still further along lines of considerable girth, and the very thought of Fat flying was highly humorous to his mates.

The little group broke up hurriedly as Bob looked at his watch and saw how time was slipping away.

"Back to the grind, fellows!" he cried. "We'll have another talk-fest later on."

That random conversation was one day to bear splendid fruit. The seeds had been sown which were to blossom into the keenest interest in the real, serious work of the mastery of the air. Live, sterling young fellows were in the Brighton Academy. Some of them had declared allegiance to the army, some to the navy, but now here was a stouthearted bunch of boys that had decided they would give themselves to the study of aeronautics, and lose no time about it.

The seven spent a thoughtful afternoon. It was hard indeed for any one of them to focus attention on his lessons. The newness of the idea had to wear off first. After class hours they met again and went off by themselves to a quiet spot on the cool, shady campus. Seated in a circle on the grass, they talked long and earnestly of ways and means for commencing their study of air-machines and airmen systematically.

"This," said Jimmy Hill with a sigh of pure satisfaction, "is team-work.

My father said this morning that team-work counts most in this war.

If our team-work is good we will get on all right."

Team-work it certainly proved to be. It was astonishing, as the days passed, how much of interest one or another of the seven could find that had to do with the subject of flying. They took one other boy into their counsels. Louis Deschamps was asked to join them and did so with alacrity, it seemed to lend an air of realism to their scheme to have the French boy in their number.

Dicky Mann's father had taken almost as great an interest in the idea as had Dicky himself, and Mr. Mann's contributions were of the utmost value.

Days and weeks passed, as school-days and school-weeks will. Looking back, we wonder sometimes how some of those interims of our waiting time were bridged. The routine work of study and play had to be gone through with in spite of the preoccupation attendant on the art of flying, as studied from prosaic print. It was a wonder, in fact, that the little group from the boys of the Brighton Academy did not tire of the researches in books and periodicals. They learned much. Many of the articles were mere repetitions of something they had read before. Some of them were obviously written without a scrap of technical knowledge of the subject, and a few were absolutely misleading or so overdrawn as to be worthless. The boys gradually came to judge these on their merits, which was in itself a big step forward.

The individual characteristics of the boys themselves began to show. Three of them were of a real mechanical bent. Jimmy Hill, Joe Little and Louis Deschamps were in a class by themselves when it came to the details of aeroplane engines. Joe Little led them all. One night he gave the boys an explanation of the relation of weight to horsepower in the internal-combustion engine. It was above the heads of some of his listeners. Fat Benson admitted as much in so many words.

"Where did you get all that, anyway?" asked Fat in open dismay.

"It's beyond me," admitted Dicky Mann.

"Who has been talking to you about internal combustion, anyway?" queried Bob Haines, whose technical knowledge was of no high order, but who hated to confess he was fogged.

"Well," said Joe quietly, "I got hold of that man Mullens that works for Swain's, the motor people. He worked in an aeroplane factory in France once, he says, for nearly a year. He does not know much about the actual planes themselves, but he knows a lot about the Gnome engine. He says he has invented an aeroplane engine that will lick them all when he gets it right. He is not hard to get going, but he won't stay on the point much. I have been at him half a dozen times altogether, but I wanted to get a few things quite clear in my head before I told you fellows."

The big airdrome that was to be placed on the Frisbie property gradually took a sort of being, though everything about it seemed to progress with maddening deliberation. Ground was broken for the buildings. Timber and lumber were delayed by Far Western strikes, but finally put in an appearance. A spur of railway line shot out to the site of the new flying grounds. Then barracks and huge hangars—-the latter to house the flying machines—-began to take form.

At first no effort was made to keep the public from the scene of the activity, but as time went on and things thereabouts took more tangible form, the new flying grounds were carefully fenced in, and a guard from the State National Guard was put on the gateways. So far only construction men and contractors had been in evidence. Such few actual army officers as were seen had to do with the preparation of the ground rather than with the Flying Corps itself. The closing of the grounds woke up the Brighton boys to the possibility of the fact that they might be shut out when flying really commenced. A council of war immediately ensued.

"A lot of good it will have done us to have watched the thing get this far if, when the machines and the flying men come, we can't get beyond the gates," said Harry Corwin.

"I don't see what is going to get us inside any quicker than any other fellows that want to see the flying," commented Archie Fox dolefully.

"What we have got to get is some excuse to be in the thing some way," declared Bob Haines. "If we could only think of some kind of job we could get inside there—-some sort of use we could be put to, it would be a start in the right direction."

Cudgel their brains as they would, they could not see how it was to be done, and they dispersed to think it over and meet on the morrow.

Help came from an unexpected source. After supper that night Harry Corwin happened to stay at home. Frequently he spent his evenings with some of the fellows at the Academy, but he had discovered a book which made some interesting comments on warping of aeroplane wings, and he stayed home to get the ideas through his head, so that he might pass them on to the other boys. Mr. and Mrs. Corwin and Harry's sister, his senior by a few years, were seated in the living room, each intent on their reading, when the bell rang and the maid soon thereafter ushered in a tall soldier, an officer in the American Army. The gold leaf on his shoulder proclaimed him a major, and the wings on his collar showed Harry, at least, that he was one of the Flying Corps.

The officer introduced himself as Major Phelps, and said he had promised Will Corwin, in France, that he would call on Will's folks when he came to supervise the new flying school at Brighton. Mr. Corwin greeted the major cordially, and after introducing Mrs. Corwin and Harry's sister Grace, presented Harry, with a remark that sent the blood flying to the boy's face.

"Here, Major," said Mr. Corwin, "is one of the Flying Squadron of the Brighton Academy."

The major was frankly puzzled. "Have you a school of flying here, then?" he asked as he took Harry's hand.

"Not yet, sir," said Harry with some embarrassment.

"That is not fair, father," said Grace Corwin, who saw that Harry was rather hurt at the joke. "The Brighton boys are very much interested in aviation, and some time ago seven or eight of them banded together and have studied the subject as hard and as thoroughly as they could. See this "—-and she reached for the book Harry had been reading—-"This is what they have been doing instead of something much less useful. There is not one of them who is not hoping one day to be a flyer at the front, and they have waited for the starting of flying at the new grounds with the greatest expectations. I don't think it is fair to make fun of them. If everyone in the country was as eager to do his duty in this war it would be a splendid thing."

Grace was a fine-looking girl, with a handsome, intelligent face. When she talked like that, she made a picture good to look upon. Harry was surprised. Usually his sister took but little account of his activities. But this was different. With her own brother Will fighting in France, and another girl's brother Will a doctor in the American Hospital at Neuilly, near Paris, Grace was heart and soul with the Allies. Harry might have done much in other lines without attracting her attention, but his keenness to become a flier at the front had appealed to her pride, and she felt deeply any attempt to belittle the spirit that animated the boys, however remote might be the possibility of their hopes being fulfilled.

Major Phelps listened to the enthusiastic, splendid, wholesome girl with frank admiration in his eyes. Harry could not have had a better champion. First the major took the book. Glancing at it, he raised his brows. "Do you understand this?" he asked.

"I think so, sir," answered Harry.

"It is well worth reading," said the major as he laid it down. Then he stepped toward Harry and took his hand again. "Your sister is perfectly right, if your father will not mind my saying so. I have been attached to the British Flying Corps in France for a time, and I saw mere boys there who were pastmasters of scout work in the air. The game is one that cannot be begun too young, one almost might say. At least, the younger a boy begins to take an interest in it and really study it, the better grasp he is likely to have of it. I am thoroughly in agreement with your sister that no one should discourage your studies of flying, and if I can do anything to help while I happen to be in this part of the world, please let me know. You look like your brother Will, and if you one day get to be the flier that he is, as there is no reason in the world you should not do, you will be worth having in any flying unit."

Harry was struck dumb for the moment. This was the first tangible evidence that the plans of the boys were really to bear fruit, after all. He stammered a sort of husky "Thank you," and was relieved to find that Major Phelps mention of Will had drawn the attention from everything else for the moment. The Corwins had to hear all about the older boy, whose letters contained little except the most interesting commonplaces.

The major, it is true, added but little detail of Will's doings, except to tell them that he was a full-fledged flying man and was doing his air work steadily and most satisfactorily. His quiet praise of Will brought a flush of pride to Grace's cheek, and the major wished he knew of more to tell her about her brother, as it was a pleasure to talk to so charming and attentive a listener.

At last he rose to take his departure, and the Corwins were loud in their demands that he should come and see them often. As the major stepped down from the piazza Harry grasped his courage in both hands and said:

"Major Phelps, may I ask you a question?"

"Certainly," said the major genially. "What is it?"

"Well, sir," began Harry, "we Brighton boys have been wondering how we can get inside the new airdrome. Summer vacation is coming, and we could all—-the eight of us, in our crowd—-arrange to stay here after the term closes. We want to be allowed inside the grounds, and to have a chance to learn something practical. We would do anything and everything we were told to do, sir."

"Hum," said the major. "Let me think. You boys can be mighty useful in lots of ways. I'll tell you what I will do. Find out whether or not your friends would care to get some sort of regular uniform and take on regular work and I will speak to the colonel about it when he comes. I think he will be here to-morrow or next day. Things are getting in shape, and we will be at work in earnest soon. The colonel is a very nice man, and when he hears that you boys are so eager to get into the game maybe he will not object to your being attached regularly to the airdrome for a while. You might find that the work was no more exciting than running errands or something like that. Are you all of pretty good size? There might be some useful things to do now and again that would take muscle."

"I am about the same size as most of the rest," replied Harry.

"You look as if you could do quite a lot," laughed the major, as he walked down the path, leaving behind him a boy who was nearer the seventh heaven of delight than he had ever been before.

Before the end of the week the colonel came. The boys had their plans cut and dried. Harry's sister Grace had taken an unusual interest in them, and had advised them wisely as to uniforms. Major Phelps seemed interested in them, too, in a way. At least, he called at the Corwin home more than once and talked to Grace about that and other things.

Colonel Marker was rather grizzled and of an almost forbidding appearance to the boys. They feared him whole-heartedly the moment they laid eyes on him. His voice was gruff and he had a habit of wrinkling his brows that had at times struck terror into older hearts than those of the Brighton boys. But he was a very kindly man, nevertheless, in spite of his bluff exterior.

Major Phelps told him about the eight lads, borrowing, perhaps, some of Grace Corwin's enthusiasm for the moment, and the colonel was favorably impressed from the start with what he called "a mighty fine spirit." He thumped his fist on the table at which he sat when the major told him of the boys and their hopes, and said explosively:

"Wish there were more like them in every town out here. We are too far from the actual scene of war. Some people who are a lot older and who should have a lot more realization of what we need and must have before this war is over might take a good lesson from such youngsters. I would like to see them."

That settled it. When the colonel took a thing up he adopted it absolutely. In a day or so he would be talking of the little band of Brighton boys as if the original project had been his from the very start. "Boy aviation corps? Why not. Good for them. Can find them plenty to do. When they get to the right size we can put 'em in the service. Why not? Good to start young. Of course it is. Splendid idea. Must be good stuff in 'em. Of course there is. Send 'em to me. Why not?"

Thus, before the boys were brought under the colonel's eye he had really talked himself into an acceptance of the major's idea. The morning he saw them, a little group of very eager and anxious faces—-bright, intelligent, fine faces they were, too—-he said without delay: "I have a use for you boys. I have thought of something for you to do. Get some sort of rig so I can tell you when I see you, and come to me again and I will set you at work."

Not long after, vacation time had come, and with it the new uniforms, in neat, unpretentious khaki. Garbed in their new feathers and "all their war paint," as Mr. Mann called it, they reported at the airdrome main gate just as the first big wooden crate came past on a giant truck. Inside that case, every boy of them knew, was the first flying machine to reach the new grounds. They felt it an omen.

A few minutes later they were in the austere presence of Colonel Marker, who was frankly pleased with their soldierly appearance and the quiet common-sense of their uniforms, which bore no fancy additions of any sort.

Grace Corwin had seen to that, though more than one furtive suggestion from one boy or another had to be overruled. Bob Haines thought the letters "B.B." on the shoulders would vastly help the effect. Crossed flags on the right sleeve would have suited Dicky Mann better. Fat Benson's voice was raised for brass buttons. Jimmy Hill's pretensions ran to a gilt aeroplane propellor for the front of each soft khaki hat. But Grace was firm. "No folderols," was her dictum. They were banded together for work, not for show. Let additions come as the fruit of service, if at all. And she had her way. Grace usually did.

"Glad to see you, boys. You will report to the sergeant-major, who will take a list of your names, assign you your duties, and arrange your hours of work. I am afraid there is no congressional grant from which to reward you for your services by a money payment, but if you do your work well, such as it is, I will keep an eye on you and see if I cannot put you in the way of learning as much as you can about the air service."

That was their beginning. They saluted, every one, turned smartly and filed out. Bob Haines, the tallest of the group and the acknowledged leader, was the only one to answer the colonel. Bob said, "Thank you, sir," as he saluted. They looked so strong and full of life and hope that the tears welled to the colonel's eyes as he watched them tramp out of his room. He had seen much war, had the colonel. "It's a shame that such lads will have to pay the great price, many of 'em," he sighed, "before the Hun is brought to his knees. But it's a fine thing to be a boy." The colonel rose stiffly and sighed. "I would give a lot to be in their shoes, with all the hardship and horror that may lie in front of them if this war keeps on long enough," he mused to himself. "It's a fine thing to be a boy."

Out went the eight Brighton boys to the sergeant-major, their work begun. They too felt it a fine thing to be boys, though their feeling was just unconscious, natural, effervescent——the sparkle of the real wine of youth and health and clean, brave spirit.

CHAPTER II

FIRST STEPS

A month after the Brighton boys had commenced their duties at the airdrome at the old Frisbie place, they would have been missed by more than one person about the camp if they had failed to put in an appearance some morning. It was astonishing to see how much routine work could pile up around the headquarters' offices.

The machines arrived in some numbers. One by one they were unpacked from their great crates and set up, then wheeled into their respective places in the broad hangars which had been built to house them.

The first one of the Brighton boys to settle himself into a regular billet was Fat Benson. He had been watching the uncrating of box of spare engine parts one afternoon when no specific job claimed him for the moment, and fell into conversation with the short, stocky sergeant who was to be the store keeper. The sergeant was tired and worried.

He had counted a consignment of sparking plugs twice and obtained a different total each time. Worse, neither of his totals tallied with the figures on the consignment sheet. He was fast losing his temper.

Fat was of most placid, unruffled temperament. He saw that trouble was toward, and was about to walk away and avoid proximity to the coming storm when he thought: "This may be a chance to help." He turned and said to the sergeant: "If you like, I will count those plugs for you while you sort out the spanners from the other crate."

"Good boy!" at once said the sergeant. "I have got to a point where those little red pasteboard boxes sort of run together, and I couldn't count them correctly to save my life. If you can make them come out to suit this consignment number they have sent with the plugs you will be a real help, I can tell you."

Henry set to work with a will, and not only checked the number of spark plugs, which he found to be correct, but at the sergeant's direction began placing them in neat piles on the shelf of the store-room that had been set aside for plugs of that type. He was in the middle of this task when who should come by but the sergeant-major!

"Hello!" exclaimed that worthy, who was nothing if not a martinet, "who told you to be puttering about here?"

Before Fat could answer, the stores sergeant spoke up. "This man is giving me a hand, and I need it," he said. "If you don't need him for something else to-day I wish you would let him stay with me. I am supposed to have a couple of soldiers detailed for this job, but I haven't seen anything of them yet. Why can't I have this man?"

Fat seemed to grow bigger than ever round the chest as he heard himself referred to as "this man." That was getting on, sure enough. More, he was mightily pleased that someone really wanted him.

"I guess you can have him if you want him," answered the sergeant-major. "Have you anything else to do to-day, Benson?"

"Not that I know about," was Fat's reply.

"Stay here, then, until the sergeant is through with you."

That night the stores sergeant suggested that Fat come to him next day. The stores were just starting, and the work of setting things in their proper places was far from uninteresting. The boy took a real delight in his new task; and when, three days later, the sergeant-major called into the stores on his way past and said to the stores sergeant, "Are you going to keep Benson here for good?" the stores sergeant replied without hesitation, "I sure am."

To have been among the stores from the time they were first unpacked, and to have assisted in the work of first placing them where they belonged, gave Fat a sort of sense of proprietorship. Stores still poured in every day or so. The two soldiers who were to help at last made their appearance, but neither of them seemed to particularly appeal to the stores sergeant, who was by that time depending more than he realized upon the quick intelligence and persistent application of his big-bodied boy assistant.

Fat's prime chance came at the end of the first fortnight, when the stores sergeant was kept in bed for a few days from unusually severe after-effects of vaccination. The pair of soldiers had not been in the new stores sufficiently long nor taken keen enough interest in them to be of much use except when working under direction. So the real storekeeper was Fat for the interim. The sergeant-major discovered the fact and reported it casually to Major Phelps, who spoke to the colonel about it. Both of these officers had their hands very full at that time, and both of them had felt the blessing of having the ever-ready and ever-willing Brighton boys always on tap, as it were, to run quick errands and be eyes and feet for anyone that required an extra pair of either.

It was a source of gratification to Colonel Marker that the boys were doing well; and that one of their number had worked his way into the organization of the camp unostentatiously, on his own merits, pleased the colonel immensely. He even went so far as to stop in the stores on his way to dinner and say a kindly word to Fat, whose coat buttons seemed ready to burst in consequence.

Thereupon Fat became a fixture in the stores, studying carefully everything that came through his hands, until at length he knew at a glance what each part or store might be, and whether it was in good condition or not when received.

The dark French boy, Louis Deschamps, was a general favorite. So much so, in fact that he could have had almost any job that it lay in the sergeant-major's power to offer him. One day Louis casually mentioned that he wished he could get nearer the engine work, and the sergeant-major at once decided the boy should have his wish.

No finer fellow on the grounds could be found than the big Scot, Macpherson, who was head engine hand of the first lot of mechanics to arrive at the airdrome. Macpherson talked little unless he was speaking to some prime favorite, when he became most voluble. The sergeant-major and Mac were cronies. Consequently it took little laying together of heads before the sergeant-major went before the colonel one day and asked if Louis Deschamps could be spared from headquarters to go and give Macpherson a hand as helper.

The colonel smiled. He knew what was in the wind. The Scot knew well where he could obtain helpers in plenty if he needed them. But Colonel Marker was as ready to help the Brighton boys as was the sergeant-major, so he smilingly acquiesced, and the next morning Louis came to camp attired in a suit of blue dungarees over his khaki.

In ten days' time Macpherson had taken the French lad to his heart, and was never so happy as when working away with him over a refractory engine and chatting along in a seemingly never-ending stream of engine small-talk. All of which was meat and drink to Louis, and was rapidly acquainting him with much that it would otherwise have taken him years of experience to acquire.

Joe Little and Jimmy Hill had a council of war with Louis Deschamps one night. These three were fast growing to be closer than brothers. What one of them had he was anxious the other two should share at once.

"I think I can see my way to get you fellows working in the hangars,"

Louis said.

"Mac will help us. I never saw such a good friend. I told him you fellows were anxious to get closer to the planes and he is turning it over in his mind. He will have a scheme soon, and when he does, it will go through all right."

Macpherson had a scheme, but just how and when to try to put it into operation was the question. He had a talk with Parks, the head instructor, one afternoon, and told Parks about the Brighton boys and their keenness to learn more about flying.

"You could do with those kids," said Mac "They are really too big by now to be called kids, as a matter of fact. Why, they will be flying soon themselves. Why don't you ask the major if you can't have two of them down here to help clean and tune up the school machines? It is a bit irregular, but so is their being here at all. I don't see why, if the Old Man can use them around the offices, we can't have a couple of them here. I have had the young Frenchman here with me now for some time, and he is worth a lot to me. He says two others, one named Hill and the other Little, want to get down to the hangars. Be a good chap and ask the major about it."

Parks did. The major was very busy at the time, and said, "I guess so," and let the matter go at that. Parks passed that laconic permission on to the sergeant-major, and the two boys reported to Parks forthwith.

That left Bob Haines, Harry Corwin, Archie Fox and Dicky Mann at headquarters to be generally useful. They had come to be on the best of terms with the sergeant-major, and when they pointed out to him that the three boys in the hangars were "having all the fun," he suggested that he so assign them to duty that but two of them would be "on" at the same time. Thus when Bob and Dicky Mann were standing ready for whatever might be required of them, Harry and Archie were free to spend their time in the hangars, where the sergeant-major could lay his hand on them in case of sudden calls.

Thus the summer was not far advanced before the Brighton boys were in the very thick of the flying game, not as onlookers, but as parts of the machine into which the various component parts of the camp and its numerous units were rapidly becoming merged.

If they had not tried to learn, the Brighton boys must have picked up some general information about aeroplanes and flying. With their special eagerness they were rapidly becoming well acquainted with most details of the work of the airmen. No casual word in their hearing fell on barren ground. When one of them mastered a new idea, he passed it on to the others.

None of the boys studied the machines themselves more devotedly than did Harry Corwin. Close application to many a dry volume bore good fruit. He felt he could set up a Farman type biplane by himself.

One morning Harry was standing beside a monoplane of the Bleriot type, which had come from somewhere as an old school machine, and had not been much in demand owing to the fact that no other monoplanes were in evidence at the camp, when an army airman, an entire stranger to Harry, came out of the hangar and glanced at the engine in evident preparation for a flight.

The airman was about to start the engine when Harry noticed that the elevator control wires were crossed. Whoever had attached them had done so mistakenly. Harry could hardly believe the evidence of his eyes, yet there it was, undeniable. Stepping forward, he said to the airman: "Excuse me, but your control wires are not right."

The flying man was little more than a novice, and sufficiently young to resent interference on the part of one obviously younger than himself. Besides, he had connected up those control wires himself. He glanced hurriedly at the terminals, and seeing that they were apparently secure, thought the boy beside him must be mistaken. He missed the crossed wires. He said to Harry, with just a suspicion of superciliousness, "Oh, she is quite O.K., thanks," and started his engine and sprang into his seat as the plane moved off across the meadow.

Harry stood watching the receding plane with something akin to consternation in his heart. Naturally shy, he did not think of pressing his opinion, but he knew trouble was in store for the young airman, though in just what form it would come he could not figure out. The monoplane had not gone far along the grass before the flier tried to raise it. As the machine did not answer properly to the elevator, he thought something must have stuck, and jerked the lever as if to free it. Afterwards the airman was not clear as to just what happened.

Harry could see the airman was trying some maneuver, and as he looked, the plane rose nose first from the ground, almost perpendicularly and then took an odd nose-dive head into the ground. The plane was not many feet from the earth when it dived, but was far enough up to come to the ground with a bad crash. Harry could see a dash of white spray in the sunlight as the gasoline splashed upward at the moment of the smash. The monoplane heeled over and the pilot went out of sight behind the wreckage. The graceful white tail stood high in air.

Running as fast as he could, Harry got to the scene of the accident before the airman had risen from the ground. The strap which had held him into his seat had burst, and he had suffered a nasty spill. Investigation showed, however, that he was but little the worse, save for the shock and the fright. He was as pale as a sheet. Harry helped him to his feet and assisted him to take stock of his injuries. By the time they had discovered that no bones were broken and the bruises the young fellow had sustained were quite superficial, Parks, the head instructor, dashed up in a motor car. As he leaped out beside the wrecked plane, there was a frown on his face. "Another smash?" he queried.

Harry learned later that the young airman had already smashed up two machines that week before demolishing the old monoplane.

"What was wrong this time?" Parks spoke sharply.

Without hesitation the young pilot answered: "I must have hitched the old girl up wrong, some way. This friend here," nodding toward Harry, "was good enough to tell me before I started that I had mussed things up before I got into her. I was a fool not to have listened to him, but," and he paused, smiling, "but he looked pretty young to be giving advice. I wish now I had listened to him."

Parks turned to Harry. "You knew where the trouble was?"

"The control wires were crossed," Harry answered simply.

"You noticed that, did you?" continued Parks. "When have you seen this type of plane before?"

"This one is the only one I have ever seen," was Harry's reply. "I have read up on this type, though, quite a bit. I had a book that contained an awful lot about this particular sort of machine, and I could almost put one together. It's easy enough to see crossed wires if your eye happens to light on them."

"Yes," said Parks. "It's easy enough if you have the right sort of an eye. That's the real question. You are one of those boys from Brighton Academy, are you not? Are you in the same bunch that Hill and Little came from? If you are, I guess I can use you in the way I am using them. Would you like to get some practical experience round the hangars? You youngsters seem to be under the chief's eye, from what I hear, and I understand he wants to see you all get a chance to push on."

"We all want to get into the hangars when we can be spared from our regular work," answered Harry. "There are four of us left, at the headquarters' offices, and whether or not they want us to stay there I don't know."

"Humph!" Parks had not great respect for anyone around an airdrome who was not intimately connected with the actual flying. "Lot of good you will be doing there. If they want to see you boys amount to something, why don't they let me have a chance to see what's in you? Fellows who know at a glance that elevator wires are crossed ought to be encouraged. That's my view." Parks left the subject and turned his attention to the bruised pilot, who came in for a curtain lecture. Harry Corwin busied himself with trying to ascertain the extent of the damage to the wrecked plane. As Parks finished talking to the pilot he stepped to Harry's side and asked: "What is left of her?"

"Plenty," said Harry. "She will need a new propellor and her running gear is crumpled up badly, but I doubt very much if the planes are damaged, and I don't see that the engine has suffered." Park's critical eye ran over the wreck and he nodded. Without further comment he jumped into his car. As it started away he said: "Don't bother with the old girl any further. I will send a gang out to tend to her. I will see if a chance won't come along soon to get you boys into better jobs, if you want them."

"Want them?" said Harry. "I should think we do."

But Parks was a very busy man, and as the work at the new air camp increased he found his hands so full that his promise to Harry was for the time being crowded out of his mind.

The four boys held at headquarters chafed a little, but were careful to keep the fact to themselves. Archie Fox felt it most keenly of all, for he was very fond of Jimmy Hill, and thought it hard fate indeed that took Jimmy away from him. Jimmy was learning rapidly. He had made friends with one of the instructor pilots, a little man named Reece, who spent much time tuning up and going over the school machines.

Reece was never idle, never quiet. An hour in which nothing had been done was to him an hour wasted. If he had nothing else to do he would go over work just completed and make sure it had been done well. In consequence, Reece had few accidents, and rarely suffered delays and waits while something was being "put right." Jimmy appreciated this quality in Reece, and saw its results.

By tuning his inclinations and point of view with that of the instructor, Jimmy got into very close touch with the little man, who was never tired of answering questions and making explanations. Reece had been for some years working for one or another of the crack international fliers who traveled in various parts of the world. He had no ambition to become a star himself, but knew most of the well-known airmen of two continents, and contained a store—-house of anecdotes about them and their doings.

Jimmy always walked or rode home with Archie when he could, and much of their time on Sundays was spent together. The colonel had from the first insisted that they should have the Sundays to themselves and they had got into the habit of going to church each Sunday morning in uniform, with the army men, who always turned out in some force. Sunday afternoons generally found them at the airdrome, and often they might be found at work, but they were considered free to do as they chose. These Sunday afternoons were of great value to Archie, for Jimmy Hill, whether working or not, never failed to give Archie a sort of resume of what he had picked up during the week.

One Thursday afternoon the colonel was making a round of the hangars. Archie was on duty with him, accompanying him as a sort of extra orderly, the soldier orderly having been sent to the town with a message.

As they passed down the front of the hangars the colonel turned to watch one of the pupils trying his first "solo," or flight by himself, not far away. "Handles her nicely," he said, half to himself. Then, turning to Archie, he added: "How would you like to be up there in that machine?"

To his surprise Archie looked very thoughtful and shook his head soberly before he replied: "I hardly know, sir."

"What!" said the colonel. "Have I found one of you Brighton boys that is not anxious to fly?"

"I am anxious enough to fly. It's the machine I was thinking about."

"What's the matter with the machine?"

"I don't know if anything is the matter with her, but that is the old biplane they call the 'bad bus.' She has given more than one man a spill, sir. Everything goes well with her for a while and then she plays a trick on someone. Last time I saw her cutup she side-slipped without any explanation for it. Some of us have got the idea that she has always got to be watched for sideslip. I would not mind going up in her after I had learned to fly, but she would not be my choice for my first solo."

"Bless my soul!" exclaimed Colonel Marker. "You talk as if you knew all about the different machines. You have never worked around them, have you?"

"Those of us that happen to be off duty at headquarters generally spend our spare time around the machines, and, of course, we hear the talk that goes on. I am sorry if I have said what I shouldn't, sir."

"Tut, tut!" from the colonel. "You have said nothing wrong. You may be quite right. I have known of machines that had bad habits, plenty of them. But if they let that lad take his solo in the machine it must be all right."

Ten minutes later Colonel Marker was at the back of a hangar inspecting a newly arrived scout machine of a much—-discussed type when he heard a shout from outside. A moment later a soldier came into the hangar and reported a bad smash. The colonel walked to the door. There across the meadow, was a wrecked airplane. Men were picking up the still form of the pilot beside it. Parks, seeing the colonel, pulled up in his runabout to take the colonel with him to the wreck.

"Looks bad, sir," said Parks. "They had orders not to let novices go up in that machine. I hope the boy is not badly hurt."

"Was it the 'bad bus' that smashed?" asked the colonel.

"Yes, sir. That is what some of the boys called her. She is not a really bad machine, but plays tricks."

"Did you see what she did this time?"

"Yes, sir. I was looking at her from the end hangar. I was some distance away, but I happened to have my eye on her as she crocked."

"Did she side-slip?"

"That is just what she did do." Parks glanced at Colonel Marker inquisitively. What was the colonel driving at?

"The reason I asked," said the colonel, "was on account of something one of those Brighton boys remarked to me not more than ten minutes before the smash. He said the 'bad bus'—-as he called it—-side-slipped at times unexpectedly. Those youngsters do pick things up, don't they?"

Just then they reached the scene of the accident, and both of them forgot the Brighton boys for the moment.

The machine was smashed badly and the young pilot had received a broken leg in addition to a nasty shaking.

"I think I will let that plane go," said Parks as he and the colonel drove toward the hangars. "I will just pile up the old thing and let her sit in a corner until I need her worse than I do now. She has played her last trick for a while. You were speaking of those Brighton boys, sir. What are you planning to do with them?"

"Make flyers of them some day."

"I have three of them in the hangars now. You have one at headquarters named Corwin that knows a bit for a lad. Why not let me have him?"

"The four I have at the offices are really valuable, but I suppose if they are to learn flying they had better be with you. Can you find something to do for the lot?"

"I guess so. If they are all as good as the three I have already

I can do with them."

"Well, it's rather irregular, the whole business. But they began with us when we came here, and they are just the sort of stuff, as far as I can see, that we want in this game, so the sooner we push 'em along the better, I think."

Thus it was settled. The Brighton boys were one step further on their way to membership of an air squadron at the front, far off as the front seemed to them. With Fat Benson in the stores and the other seven boys in the hangars, they felt themselves truly part and parcel of the airdrome. This feeling of responsibility was aging them, too. Already they looked years older, every one of them, than they had looked on that day in the previous spring when they had decided to study aeronautics in concert.

CHAPTER III

IN THE AIR

Bob Haines was the first of the Brighton boys to go up in an aeroplane.

It was due to no planning on his part. It was not to please him that he was taken as a passenger. One of the pilots was trying a machine new to him and came down complaining of its lack of stability on the turns.

"Any little puff that catches her sudden makes her wiggle herself in a way I have never seen another plane do. I suppose these chasers have little habits of their own, but it would take my attention off what I was doing, to have her monkeying around that way. What do you think it is?"

The instructor addressed was unable to answer. "You have been up in her. You know more than I do about her."

"Perhaps a passenger would help her," suggested another pilot.

"I don't see how." The flier shook his head. "Anyway, I would like to see how she climbs with two up. From the little I tried her out, I think she is the fastest climber I have been in anywhere. Come up for a bit, John."

"Can't," said the pilot. "About ten minutes ago the major sent word he wanted to see me at once. If I don't get a move on I will catch it." He started off in a hurry.

"Come on, Fanshaw," said the pilot, turning to the instructor.

"Not me," was the reply. "I have a swat of work. There is ballast for you, though, over there by the shed." Bob Haines was the ballast indicated. He was putting the final touches on an aeroplane propellor to which he had administered a coat of varnish.

"What lot?" queried the pilot.

"Bunch of young fellows from about here. Sort of volunteers. Idea of the colonel's, I think. Nice lot of boys. Young, but getting on fast. I have seen one of them, a French boy, quite a bit lately, and if they are all as good at locating engine trouble as he is they will go far in this game before they are old men. Ask the tall youngster. He will be tickled to death. I don't suppose he has been up before, but he will be a good passenger. Be careful and don't scare him. Don't try any stunts. Shall I sing out to him?"

"I guess so. I don't much care who it is so long as he weighs up to average, and that fellow looks pretty husky."

"Here, young fellow! You are needed here for a minute," called out

Fanshaw.

Bob trotted over to the plane at once.

"What were you at?" asked the instructor.

"Varnishing," replied Bob. "Just finished."

"This is Lieutenant Fauver. He is trying this new chaser. She is the finest thing we have seen here, and he wants to give her a spin with a passenger up. Hop in if you like."

The pilot smiled and shook Bob's hand, then added another invitation. It was hardly necessary. Bob was overjoyed. Often the boys had discussed going up, but a fair frequency of minor accidents made the officers at the camp chary about any unnecessary risks. Consequently, the Brighton boys had decided that their best plan was to say nothing about flying as passengers until someone suggested it to them. That one of them might be of any possible use as a passenger had never entered their heads.

A few moments after, the new chaser was soaring upward with a roar of engine exhaust that told of pride of power. Bob was in the snug front seat undergoing an experience whose like he had never dreamed of. His youthful imagination had often tried to picture what it would be like to be up in a swift flying-machine, but the sense of power and the exhilaration of swinging triumphantly through space gave him a new sensation.

"This," he thought, "is the greatest game of all. This is what one day I will be doing to some purpose."

His mind went out to that day when he would be guiding his own machine on a hostile errand, over the enemy's country, perhaps. The fine, high enthusiasm of youth rushed through him and his pulses beat faster as he pictured himself, a knight of the air, starting forth on a quest that might mean great danger, but would, with sufficient foresight, care and determination, result in disaster for the antagonist rather than for himself.

Higher and higher climbed the swift plane, no faltering in its stride. The beat of the engines was as rhythmical to experienced ears as the regular swing and lilt of some perfectly rendered piece of music to the ears of a master musician.

Bob noticed the country below, but was too much absorbed with his own thoughts to give much attention to details of the wonderful panorama that stretched away for miles and miles, until they had soared to a height that made blurred lines of roads and hedges far under them, and caused even houses and outbuildings to grow increasingly indistinguishable. Only the silver band of the little river, winding in graceful curves and catching the afternoon sun, remained an unfailing landmark.

Then suddenly came an abrupt silence. Bob's heart leaped to his throat. What had happened? No sooner had his inner consciousness asked the question than his common sense had answered it. The pilot had shut off the engine, of course. Already the powerful plane was heading downward over the trackless path up which it had risen, and was gliding with a soft rush of air which produced a floating sensation.

"How did you like that?" asked Lieutenant Fauver.

"Great," said Bob. Great! He wanted to say more. He wanted to explain that a new world had opened to him. That he had felt the call that would leave him restless until he, too, had mastered one of those marvelous steeds of the air, and was free to soar at will wherever he chose to direct his mount. Great! The word expressed so little. Bob thought of a dozen things to say, but heaved a big sigh of genuine content, and left them all unsaid.

Fauver was of much the same mold as Bob. He caught something of the younger boy's mood. He knew how the lad felt. His memory took him back to his own first flight. How long ago it seemed! How impressed he had been at his first real taste of the sweets of the air-game! How utterly incapable of expressing his feeling!

So he respected the frame of mind of the lad in front of him and volplaned down in silence, trying the stability of the plane by wide spirals, banking it just enough to be delightful to a passenger, without going far enough to cause the slightest apprehension or nervousness.

It was proving a priceless experience to Bob. He seemed transported to another existence. Then the earth began to come nearer. Things below took quick form. Bob realized that soon they would be landing. Just at the last he thought the ground was rising toward them at an astonishing rate. Surely this was not quite right! They must be dropping like a stone. Up, up, came the ground. Bob unconsciously braced himself for the impact. They were going to come down with a mighty smash. He held his breath and set his teeth. At the very moment when all seemed over but the crash, the graceful plane lifted its head ever so slightly, the engine started roaring again, and they glided to earth and ran along so smoothly that for the life of him Bob could not have told the exact moment the wheels touched the ground.

When they stepped out of the machine Bob did something on the spur of the moment that he laughed about afterward. He stepped to the lieutenant and put out his hand. As Fauver took it in a friendly, firm grasp Bob said: "That was the biggest experience of my life." Again that similarity of temperament between the two told Fauver something of the depth of Bob's feeling, and he said quietly: "I am glad to have given you a chance to go up, and next time you happen to be around when I am going up, if you can get away for a little while, I would be glad to have you go along. One of these days I will give you a good long flight, if I get a chance."

Bob went back to the hangar an older boy. The enthusiasm still held him close. The days would drag, now, until he could begin flying. He was sure of that.

When the other Brighton boys learned that Bob had actually been up in the air, there was a natural desire among them all to do likewise. Jimmy Hill made up his mind it would not be long before he had a flight. Adams, one of the instructors who had recently arrived, wanted a hand to help him tune up a new school machine that was fitted with dual control, i.e., that had a double set of levers so that the novice could guide the machine while the instructor had a restraining hand on them in case of emergencies. Reece, Jimmy Hill's great friend, was called away to make a test flight just as Adams spoke to him about a good helper, and told Adams that he could not do better than give Jimmy a chance to lend a hand.

"The boy will do what he is told," said Reece. "All you have to do is to explain just what you want done. He is dependable. Try him. He is a nice boy, too, and you will like to have him round."

So Jimmy worked that day and the next on the new school machine.

Finally it was ready.

"Wait till I take her up for a bit and see how she pulls and I will give you a runaround in her," said Adams to Jimmy. The instructor had been highly pleased with the way the boy had worked, and felt anxious to give him a treat.

Thus Jimmy had his first flight. Further, he was shown by Adams how to hold the controls, though he was careful to put no pressure on them. Next day Adams said, "Come on. I will show you how we start teaching flying where I come from."

Before half an hour passed Jimmy found he could "taxi," as Adams called running along the ground, quite well. That was but a beginning. Three times in the following week Adams took the boy out for a lesson; and the practical experience, though limited, gave Jimmy a very good idea of what was required of much of the adjustments and finer points of tuning up that he had learned to see Reece do in the sheds.

At last Adams made a short flight and let Jimmy handle the machine for a few moments alone, the instructor removing his hands from his control levers and leaving the job to Jimmy. It was a simple enough little flight, but Jimmy had the knowledge that he had been actually flying the machine for a time, all by himself, which pleased him beyond measure.

One of the red-letter days the Brighton boys were long to remember was that on which they first watched a new arrival to the airdrome, an experienced flier, loop the loop and nose-dive on one of the fast chasers. The whirling, darting plane seemed so completely at the mercy of the pilot that the boys were rapt in silent wonder. That exhibition of what the birdmen of to-day call real flying was a revelation to them.

It held out promise of long study and careful practice far ahead before they could hope to equal or excel the cool, modest young aviator who came down so gracefully after a series of side loops that made most of the spectators hold their breath.

Summer days passed rapidly. Joe Little and Louis Deschamps were sitting in a hangar one Sunday afternoon, chatting about a new type of battle-plane that had arrived that week.

"I could fly that bus," said Joe, "if I had a chance."

"That is just the trouble," commented Louis. "Getting the chance is what is so hard. I am tired of fussing around on those school machines they let us on now and then. What is the good of trying to fly on a plane that won't rise more than a couple of dozen feet? I have never had a chance to fly anything else. I get to thinking, working so much on real planes, that those school machines for the infant class are not fliers at all. They are a sort of cross between a flying machine and an auto."

"You are in too much of a rush," Joe admonished. "I think we are lucky to get a go in one of those now and then. Jimmy Hill goes up in that old dual-control bus with Adams, but to my mind that sort of thing is out of date. I have got the idea of lateral control as well on that school bus that Parks let me out on, as I could have got it from any of the chasers. Another go or two and I will get horizontal control down fine, and then I am ready for a real go. I can land the school bus like a bird. I am getting swelled up, Louis."

"All right. But don't get so swelled that you play the goat, Joe. I know you won't, for that matter. You are one of the careful ones, all right. But this does not get us any nearer flying a real machine."

"I wish I had a machine of my own," said Joe mournfully.

"Wishing won't get it, Joe."

"I wonder why we can't get hold of a machine that has been finished off by one of these cheerful student chaps, and still has some good stuff left in it, and get Parks to let us patch it up and get a flight on it?"

"Parks can't be all that generous of government property, old man. If a plane is worth fixing up the chief wants the rest of the use of it. If it is no good to him it would not be worth anything to us; that's the rub there."

"I've got it!" exclaimed Joe, slapping his knee. "Why not hit Parks for that old 'bad bus' that gave the young fellow the broken leg the last time it smashed? There is plenty of life left in that old girl. I wonder they haven't taken the engine out of her if they don't intend to fix her up, The engine is all right."

"Maybe the engine is out of her. Where is she?"

"Down in number twelve hangar, covered up in the corner."

"Let's go and have a look at her."

The two lads trotted off to inspect the damaged plane, which they found under a pile of canvas, just where it had been brought the day a bad side-slip had resulted in smashing it up.

"The engine is in her, sure enough," said Louis, "and it is by no means a bad type of engine either. It might have more power, but it is reliable enough. What was the matter with this bus, anyway, that made them decide to shelve her?"

Someone told me that she side-slips badly at times. I never heard why. Planes don't do things like that without there being a reason, Louis. Maybe she needs a bit of fixing that she has never had. It would be fun if we could rig her up so that she would fly properly, wouldn't it? Wonder if there is any use asking Parks?"

"Parks could only ask the colonel, I suppose. He is a real good fellow, and always seems willing to help us in every way he can. I don't see, if he does not intend to repair the 'bad bus,' why he wouldn't let us do it in our spare time, I know he would trust me to do the engine. He said the other day I could tune up an engine as well as anyone he had under him."

"You could fix up the engine easy enough," said Joe "It is the rest of the machine that would take some doing. She is in pretty rocky shape, an would want a lot replaced. Harry Corwin could help us with her. He has had a lot of work with frames lately. For that matter, I guess all the lot would help. We could come in early and get some time on her before work starts, stay a bit later at night, and most Sunday afternoons we could hammer away at her without interruption. It would be rather fun to have the seven of us trying to show what we have learned and putting it into practice that way. If we got the old bus right I don't think they would mind our having a flight or two on her now and then, do you?"

"Sure not," replied the French boy. "But will the colonel give us the chance?"

"We will know before many days have passed."

Parks shook his head at first when the boys broached the project to him. "I don't think the colonel will agree," was his comment.

"I had better wait for a good time to introduce the idea. There is no telling what he might think of it. Personally, I was undecided what to do with that machine. I have just let it set there waiting till I made up my mind. I can't recommend scrapping a plane merely because it has the reputation of being unlucky. That is about all the bad name of the 'bad bus' amounts to, after all. I am not sure that you boys would not turn her out in better shape than the repair men turned her out last time. I can't see the harm in the plan."

Parks generally got his way about the hangars. Colonel Marker depended greatly on Parks' judgment, which the colonel was fond of calling "horse sense." So when the head instructor spoke to the colonel about the proposal the Brighton boys had made to repair the "bad bus" in their own time, and obtain, as a special reward for good work, permission to do a little flying on the machine when opportunity occurred, Colonel Marker felt inclined to leave the matter to Parks, and said so. That really settled it, for Parks had decided to plead the cause of the boys.

The weeks that passed were very full ones for the Brighton boys, who worked like Trojans on the machine they had undertaken to put in order. They made some mistakes, and more than once had to apply to Parks for help and advice. These he gave cheerfully. Louis and Macpherson overhauled the engine, and pronounced it in A-1 condition when it left the test bench. Every one of the boys learned much about aircraft construction, at least so far as that type of biplane was concerned, before they were through with the job.

Finally the day came when the "bad bus"—-rechristened the "boys' bus "—-was wheeled out for its trial flight after the completion of the repairs. Adams was chosen to make the trial trip, which went off without incident. He flew the big biplane six or seven hundred feet above the green carpet of the airdrome, and came down with a graceful volplane that caused the boys to feel like applauding.

"Who is next?" asked Adams as he sprang from the seat and the biplane came to rest beside the little group.

The honor was voted to Joe Little, as the originator of the idea of getting hold of the machine. Joe was not very eager to go up when it came to an actual trial of the plane. He thought he would have no difficulty in flying it, for the controls were very familiar to him, and a straight flight, or even a wide circle of the flying ground proper, offered no apparent difficulties. Joe was naturally a shy and retiring lad, and felt that he was very much in the limelight as he climbed into the seat of the biplane.

Joe got off well enough to suit the most critical instructor, and after rolling until he was quite sure of himself, he raised the elevator slightly and the machine left the ground in a most satisfactory manner.

Joe did not try to fly at a great height, but once well clear of the ground settled into his seat and started to gently turn to the left, commencing a wide circle that would land him, should he choose to come down at the end of one circuit of the grounds, at the point where the Brighton boys and Parks were watching him.

There was so little wind that it had no noticeable effect on the plane. The controls worked perfectly, and Joe felt increasingly at his ease. When he had made the first circuit he decided to continue, rise to a somewhat greater height, and come down with a nice, simple volplane at the feet of his fellows.

All continued to go well. Nothing was necessary but to watch that no sudden gust caught the plane and found its pilot unprepared. The plane was banked so slightly that he had no need to fear side-slip. He concentrated all his powers on making a fine landing. When he was ready to come down he shut off his engine and dipped the biplane slightly. She answered like a bird, and started gliding earthward delightfully, planing at a perfect angle.

While Joe was not far up, he had never flown a machine before at that height, and consequently his volplane seemed to occupy a longer time than it should have done. His fingers itched to start the engine again and raise the elevator just enough to arrest the downward swoop, and transform it into a soft glide, nicely calculated so that it would bring the wheels of the chassis into contact with the ground without any shock. He was over-keen on that landing, realizing that so many pairs of eyes were on him.

The earth came up toward him just a shade too fast to suit him. Then he decided that the right moment had come, lifted his elevator slightly, started the engine for a few turns, and wondered if he had done the thing well.

He had not.

Joe, in his anxiety and inexperience, had pulled up his machine a little too quickly. Its headway stopped, as it was still a dozen feet from the ground, along which Joe had hoped to glide gracefully to rest. The biplane hung a moment in the air, as if undecided what to do. Fortunately Joe had shut off the engine when his intuition told him all was not right. He could not tell what distance the wheels of the chassis lacked before they would rest on terra firma, but hoped against hope that they were nearer than they seemed to be.

The machine, losing all impetus, simply sat down with a bump. The chassis and the under plane smashed with a sound of ripping canvas and splintering wood. Joe had a good bump, too, but was none the worse for it physically. He stepped out of his seat before the boys could run to the wrecked biplane. They were all sympathy and eagerness to see if Joe was hurt. He had not dropped far, but had come down with such a thud that even Parks was anxious. Bob Haines was the first of the Brighton boys to reach the machine. "Are you all right, Joe?" he called out as he came up.

"Guess so," was the reply. "I feel jarred—-but look at the poor old bus! How did I do it? After all our hard work, she is completely wrecked again, and I did it." Joe felt that it would be a relief to get away from the scene of the smash, and had to down a temptation to walk off by himself. He was almost heartbroken when he thought of all the work that his mistake had undone.

"Never mind," said Parks. "Everyone has to learn. I will bet that you don't pull up short when landing another time."

Joe was not to be thus easily comforted. Sensitive to a degree, his heart entirely in his work, he was utterly disgusted with himself for having had the temerity to try the flight. What hurt most was the knowledge that the plane the Brighton boys had so looked forward to having for practice flying they could hardly hope to get otherwise for a long time to come, was hors de combat, and possibly beyond another repair.

Recognizing Joe's frame of mind, the boys grouped round the broken biplane in silence, searching their minds for a word that would give a crumb of comfort to their comrade. The more they looked over the wreck, the less they knew what to say.

As they stood there, watching Parks poking round the smashed machine, Colonel Marker came up with Major Phelps. They had not been far away when Joe had started on his experimental round of the airdrome, and had witnessed the whole episode.

"You did not do so badly until you landed," said the colonel pleasantly.

"You should have stayed up."

The boys had never before heard the colonel essay a joke, and were by no means sure that his first remark was not the preface to serious condemnation of Joe. Colonel Marker had often been heard to treat the subject of smashed machines in a manner decidedly uncomplimentary to the luckless aviator who was responsible.

Poor Joe felt his heart in his throat. A very deep feeling of shame came over him and his eyes filled with tears. His face showed real distress.

The colonel turned to Joe from an inspection of the plane and as he did so saw the boy's eyes. Colonel Marker was a kindhearted man, for all his gruff exterior, and he had, too, a great interest in the Brighton boys and their progress. He felt, the moment he realized how much to heart Joe had taken the accident, a sense of sincere sympathy for the lad.

Placing his hand on Joe's shoulder, he said: "My boy, what counts most is the way you have worked to get that old machine into flying shape, and the fact that you were ready and willing to have a shot at flying her, with all your inexperience. Those things show keenness, enthusiasm, and pluck. A flying man has to possess nerve. He has to take chances sometimes. You did the best you could do. The fact that you were inexperienced was against you, but in failing to get through without accident you gained experience. I do not care half so much about the machine as you might think. I might have left it unrepaired if you boys had not taken on the job. Don't feel so badly, my boy."

Joe had difficulty in finding his voice. "But, sir," he said in a low tone, "the boys had looked forward so much to getting a chance to learn to fly on the old bus. Now that is all knocked into a cocked hat. I feel that I have robbed them of something I can't give them again. They are too good to say so, but every one of them feels the disappointment as much as can be."

"Well," said the colonel, "there is no need for too much downheartedness on that score. Maybe I can play fairy godmother along that line. You Brighton boys have worked hard and studied hard. I have watched you. I am pleased with you. You are all big enough now to begin the game, I think, or at least you will be soon. What do you think, Major?"

"I think you are right, sir," replied Major Phelps quietly. "If any boys deserve to be taken into the service these surely do. They may be a bit on the young side, but they will be quite old enough by the time they get to France."

To France! The Brighton boys could hardly believe their ears. That casual sentence quickened every pulse. To France! The bare suggestion made them glow with anticipation.

"How do you feel about it?" asked the colonel, turning to the seven.

"Every one of us is ready to go into the service the very first day we can be taken in," answered Bob Haines. "We started with that idea in view. We all hoped some day to join up, and we think we could be of more use in the Flying Corps than anywhere else. I don't mean by that that we want to pick our jobs, sir, but we would like to get into the air service for choice."

"And a very good choice too," commented Colonel Marker. "Major Phelps, suppose you look into the individual work that each of these boys has been doing lately, and see if those under whom they have worked recommend them all. Is this the lot of them?"

"One more, sir," spoke up Bob. "Benson, sir, in the stores."

"Benson has proven to be mightily useful," said the major.

"All right," concluded the colonel. "Come on, Phelps. We must look over the ground for those new hangars. You can tell me what you find about these Brighton boys when you have finished your inquiries." They walked away together, leaving seven of the proudest and happiest boys in the world.

"Give a hand to get this wreck into the shed," said Parks. "You fellows are all right now. The old man knows well enough you boys have been doing well. That is just his way. You had better find out what your folks are going to say."

Each of the boys felt confident that the news would be well received at home. They fell to with a will and soon had the biplane moved into the shed. That night they went home in high spirits. They were boys no longer; they had become men. They pictured themselves in real service uniforms, and longed for the day when, as Major Phelps had said, they would "get to France."

Harry Corwin and Joe Little lingered for a moment at the gate of the Hill home for a final word with Jimmy, who was very much excited. "It all came out of your smash, Joe," said Harry. "The colonel might not have thought of us for a long time yet but for that. You could not have done it better if you had planned it."

Joe had gotten over the worst of his chagrin. He smiled. "I am glad it has taken the minds of you fellows off of my smash, anyway," he said.

Each family into which that news came that evening took it differently. None of the parents of the Brighton lads who heard of the colonel's promise were quite prepared for it. All thought the boys might be taken in some day, but it had seemed a long way off. Bob Haines' uncle was very proud of Bob, and telegraphed Senator Haines that Bob was going into the army as a matter of information rather than a request for permission.

Mrs. Mann was anything but glad to hear Dicky's "good news." She was a timid little woman, with a horror of all fighting. Mr. Mann took Dicky by the hand, however, and said, "God bless you, son," in a way that made Dicky feel closer to his father than he had ever been before. Jimmy Hill's mother was away from home.

Mr. Hill took the information as a matter of course. "I thought they would take you in one of these days," he remarked. "You boys ought to prove a credit to us all. I would give a lot to be as young as you are and have your chance, Jimmy. You will have to represent the family, though, I guess. They won't take men of my age, at least yet." Jimmy made up his mind then and there that he would represent his father, of whom he was intensely proud and very fond, and represent him to the very best of his ability.

Harry Corwin's folks seemed little surprised. Grace kissed him very tenderly, and his mother drew his head down and pressed his cheek close to hers. "That will take both of my boys," she said quietly. In the conversation that followed at the dinner table Harry was struck with the familiarity with which they all spoke of the possibility that the boys would be taken into the service at once. They had not discussed the matter in such detail before in his presence. Grace mentioned more than once something that "the major said," and Harry finally came to the conclusion that his people had been closer in touch with the matter than he had been. Major Phelps saw a good deal of Grace. Perhaps that had much to do with it.

The Bensons and the Foxes took the news less seriously. "I guess it will be a long time before you boys see France," said Mr. Fox. "It is the right thing, though, and if you get a chance, take it."

Louis Deschamps was to receive a bigger piece of news from his mother than he gave to her.

"Next week we leave for France, both of us," said Mrs. Deschamps. "I have not told you, Louis, for you were so happy with your work at the airdrome I wanted you to enjoy it while you could do so. You are French, my son, and thank God you are becoming old enough to take a hand in the war. When we get home I will see what can be done to place you at once in our own flying service. If you have learned much here, as I think you have, it will all come in well when you are fighting for France."

Louis was overjoyed. He liked his comrades of the school, but he was, after all, a French boy and had a French boy's heart. More, he had a French mother, with a French mother's devotion to her country and her country's cause.

"For France!" an expression often heard in the Deschamps' household, meant more than mere words could utter. All the fine, high resolve; all the passionate belief in the justice of the French cause; all the stern determination that the war must be won, whatever the cost—-all that went to make the magnificent French women of to-day the splendid heroines they have shown themselves to be, was deeply rooted in Mrs. Deschamps. Her husband in the trenches, she might well have begrudged her only son, so young and such a mere boy in all his ways. Not she. She was a true mother of France. The highest sacrifice was not too great to make for the republic.

So Louis was soon to leave the Brighton boys, to go on to France ahead of them, and to be enrolled in his own army, by the side of which his American school chums hoped one day to be fighting a common enemy.

Another mother of one of the Brighton boys was of the same heroic mold as the brave French woman. Joe Little's widowed mother took the news calmly. She had felt it would come one day. Her mind went back, as it had done frequently after the boys had commenced their work at the airdrome, to the days of the short Spanish-American war. Joe's father, impulsive, had joined the colors at the first call and gone to Cuba. Mrs. Little's only brother, very dear to her, had volunteered, too, and was in the First Expedition to the Philippines. Neither had come back. War had taken so much from Mrs. Little, and left her so hard a bed to lie upon, that it seemed cruel that she should be asked for still more sacrifice. She had fought it all out in the quiet of her bedchamber, where, night after night, she had prayed long and earnestly for guidance and strength and courage.

Well Mrs. Little knew that if she told Joe the truth about her finances and what his going would mean to her she could doubtless influence him to stay and care for her. There were many others who could be sent, who did not, could not, mean so much to those they would leave behind. Joe was all she had. She was growing old, and her little store of money was dwindling surely if slowly.

By the time Joe came home that night and told her of what the colonel had said, Mrs. Little had steeled herself to give her boy to her country and humanity. It cost her dear, but she set her teeth and placed her offering on the altar of what she had come to believe her duty, with a brave, patient smile in her eyes, in spite of the clutch at her heartstrings.

"Splendid, Joe," she said with what enthusiasm she could put into her words. "You are glad, aren't you, dear?"

"Not glad, mother darling." Joe placed his arm around her slender waist tenderly. They were very close, these two. "Not glad. That does not express it. I couldn't be glad to go away and leave you. Though, for that matter, you will be all right. I feel sort of an inspiration I can't explain. It is all so big. It seems so necessary that I should go, and I felt that I should be so utterly out of it if I did not go one day. When the colonel spoke that way it seemed like a sort of fulfillment of something that had to come, whether or no. I might call it fate, but that does not describe it quite. It is bigger than fate. It sounds silly, mother, but it is a sort of exaltation, in a sense. It had to come, and I feel it is almost a holy thing to me."

Joe's mother put her two hands on his shoulders. Her eyes were moist, but her courage never faltered. "Joe, such boys as you are could not stay at home. You are your father's son, dear."

"And my mother's," said Joe soberly. "It is from you I get the strength to want to do my duty, and I will not forget it when the strain comes. I will always have your face in front of me to lead me on, mother."

CHAPTER IV

OFF FOR THE FRONT

Months passed. The training of the Brighton boys went on steadily after they entered the service until each one of the six of them that were still at the home airdrome was a highly efficient flier and well-grounded in the construction of air-machines as well.

Louis Deschamps had gone, with his mother, to France. Fat Benson had been passed on to a more important job. His work had been so thorough in the stores department that he was now being used as an inspector, traveling over half a dozen states, visiting all sorts of factories that were being broken-in gradually to turn out the necessary aeroplane parts in ever-increasing quantities as the war progressed.

Then came the day when the contingent into which the Brighton boys had been drafted started, at last, for France. Final good-bys were said, last parting tears were shed, the cheers and Academy yells at the station died into the distance as the train pulled out, and the six young airmen, proud in the security of full knowledge that they were no novices, were truly "off for the front."

The days of embarkation, the dash across the Atlantic, and the landing in France came in due sequence. They had expected some excitement on the ocean voyage. The group of transports, of which their ship was one, steamed warily eastward, convoyed by a flotilla of grim destroyers, swift, businesslike, determined. Extra precautions were taken in the submarine zone; but none of the German sea wolves rose to give battle with the American ships.

The coming into port, too, was less exciting than they had thought it would be. The French people who were grouped along the quayside cheered and waved, but the incoming American contingents were arriving with such regularity that the strangeness had worn away. America was in the war to do her utmost. France knew that well by the time the Brighton boys crossed the ocean. The welcome was no less warm, but there was no element of novelty about it.

A troop train, consisting mainly of cattle trucks, puffed away from the coast town next morning, and attached to it were the cars containing the new air squadron. Late that night it had reached one of the huge airdromes, the vastness of which unfolded itself to the astonished gaze of the boys at daybreak of the morning after. They had not dreamed that such acres and acres of hangars existed along the whole front. The war in the air assumed new proportions to them. They were housed in huts, warm and dry, if not palatial.

During the day, given leave to wander about the airdrome, the six Brighton boys took a stroll in company, eager to inspect at close quarters the latest types of flying machines.

"These airplanes are stronger than any we have ever seen," remarked

Joe Little, as they paused before a new-type French machine.

"Yes," cheerily commented an aviator—-a clean-cut young Englishman—- who was grooming the graceful plane. "This very one crashed into the ground two weeks ago while going at over sixty miles an hour. She is so strongly built that she was not hurt much and the pilot escaped without a scratch. This is what we call a 'hunter.' She has an unbeaten record for speed—-can show a clean pair of heels to anything in the air. She has tremendous power; and the way she can climb into the clouds—-my word!"

"Is she easy to fly?" asked Dicky Mann.

"Not bad," was the answer. "The high speed makes for a bust-up once in a while. A pilot who gets going over one hundred and fifteen miles an hour, and yanks his machine up to six thousand feet in seven minutes, as he can do on this type of plane, and then drops straight down from that elevation, as the 'hunter' fellows have to do sometimes, puts a mighty big strain on his bus. Little by little this sort of thing dislocates important parts. Of course the pursuing game makes a pilot put his machine into all sorts of positions. He has to jump at the other chap, sometimes, at an angle of ninety degrees. I have known of cases where the air pressure caused by such a drop has been so great that the planes of one of these 'hunters' have been broken off with a snap."

"Jiminy!" ejaculated Dicky.

At this the aviator laughed, saying smilingly: "Accidents of some sort take place here several times a day. If they didn't we would not get on so fast either in the study of aeroplane construction or the art of flying itself. Accidents tell us lots of things. Between studying accidents and watching for Boche ideas, especially when we get hold of one of their late machines, we are never standing still at this game, I can tell you."

"Do you get many German planes?" asked Jimmy Hill.

"We down lots of 'em, but we don't get many—-which is different," and the aviator smiled. "You see the Boche fliers stay their side, mostly, and when we drop one he goes down among his own lot. Now the hostile hunters for instance, rarely go over our lines. Their business apparently is to remain over their own territory. That is their plan. They are brave enough. But the Germans look to their hunters chiefly to prevent our observers from doing their work. They wait for our observation machines where they know the observers must come. That is their game. Just get some of the fellows who have been over recently, when you get up front a bit, to tell you how the new Fokkers hide themselves and pounce on our lot.

"Maybe the Boches look at it this way: if they have their fight at their base of operations, over their own lines, and win out, they may make a prisoner; if the machine is not destroyed, that may be utilized. If their man gets put out of commission we don't get the beaten machine and therefore cannot learn their latest construction dodges from it. It's a different plan of action. We go right out over the German lines with our hunters and tackle their observers, who do their reconnaissances from a bit back of their lines. Only in the very first part of the war, when the Germans outnumbered us in fliers to an enormous extent, did they try to do much from our top-side. Nowadays we do our observing daily from well over the enemy's lines; and the Germans do most of theirs from well on their own side. It's a different way of looking at it."

"Surely our way must be more efficient," said Joe Little.

"We think so," assented the aviator. "We know more of their lines than they can possibly know of ours. For the rest of this war I guess we will have to do so. We are going forward from now on, and the Teutons are going back, and don't you forget it. We have to know their lines well, and lots of other things, such as their routes of supply and reinforcement, and their gun positions and munition dumps. Our guns look to us, too, in a way they did not look to us a year ago, even. It's a big game."

The Brighton boys walked on slowly, without comment. Yes, it was a big game, in very truth. The closer they came to it the bigger it became.

"Hello! There is a monoplane. I thought there were no monoplanes in use now," said Bob Haines as they passed a round-bodied fleet-looking machine with a single pair of wings. It was a single-seater. They walked up to it and round it, gazing admiringly at its neat lines. "What sort of a plane is this?" asked Bob of a mechanic who was standing beside the machine.

"An absolute hummer," was the reply. "Want to try her? You have to be an Ace to get into her driving seat, son."

Bob flushed, and was inclined to answer sharply, but Joe Little stepped forward and said quietly: "We have just got here from the States. Came last night. This is our first look-around, and we want to learn all we can. We did not know monoplanes were being used now. The only aeroplanes we have flown have been biplanes. Won't you tell us something about this type?"

"Certainly," said the mechanic. "I was only joking. No one can fly this sort of machine except the most experienced and best pilots. It is the fastest machine in the world. It is a Morane, and they call it a 'Monocoque.' Someone told me that the latest type German Fokker was modeled on this machine. It is a corker, but the trickiest thing to fly that was ever made. We have only got one here. I heard a French flyer say the other day that the Spad biplane was faster than this machine, but I don't believe it."

"What is an Ace?" queried Jimmy Hill.

"That term started with the French," answered the mechanic. "We use it here now, sometimes. It means a superior aviator, who has brought down five adversaries, in fair air-fight. The bringing-down business, at least so far as the exact number is concerned, is not always applied, I guess. They just call a man an Ace when he is a real graduate flyer, and gets the habit of bringing down his Boche when he goes after him."

Every conversation around that part of the world seemed to have a grim flavor. The Brighton boys were getting nearer to actual war every minute, they felt.

The boys found a row of S.P.A.D. machines not far distant. The "Spads," as the aviators called them, were fleet biplanes. They found a genial airman to tell them something of the planes, which he described as the latest type of French fighting aeroplane. "This sort has less wing surface than any machine we have had here," said the airman. "It is mighty fast. These four have just come back from a good pull of work. I think this lot were all that is left of two dozen that were attached to the B squadron just before the last big push."

"Cheerful beggar!" spoke up another pilot within earshot. "Are you trying to impress a bunch of newcomers?" He walked toward the boys. "Are you not some of the crowd that got in last night?"

"Yes," answered Bob Haines. "We're the Brighton Academy bunch. We have just come over from home."

"Do you know a fellow called Corwin?"

"I am Corwin," said Harry.

"My name is Thompson. Your brother Will was over here last week looking for you, and told me that if I was still here when you arrived I was to look you up. He may not get a chance to run over again for a bit. He is some distance away."

Harry was delighted. He introduced his companions to Thompson, who told them Will Corwin was fit and well, and had become quite famous as a flyer. Thompson promised to dine at their mess that evening. He did so, and after dinner sat and chatted about flying in general, telling the Brighton boys many things strange to them about the development of the flying service since the beginning of the war.

"I was in England in August, 1914, when the war broke out," Thompson said. "I had been interested for some time in flying; had learned to fly a machine myself, and had watched most of the big international flying meets. I knew some of the rudimentary points about aircraft, and as I had a cousin who was in the motor manufacturing business in England, I had been put fairly into touch with aeroplane engines. I don't know how much is known at home about what the French and British flying corps have done out here, but to get a fair idea of what they have accomplished one has to know something of the way both France and England were caught napping. I think it is fair to say that there was not one firm in all Great Britain at the outbreak of hostilities which had proven that it could turn out a successful aeroplane engine.

"The English War Department had what they called the Royal Aircraft Factory, where some experimental work was done, but the day war was declared the British Army had less than one hundred serviceable flying machines of all types. What proved to be the most useful plane used by the British for the first year of the war was only a blueprint when the fighting started. France was better off. She had factories that could make aero engines. But as to actual planes, three hundred would be an outside figure of the number with which France went to war.

"The use of the aeroplane in war was a subject which gave much discussion, but few people, even in the army, thought that the aeroplane would be of great service except for scouting. At the airdrome where I learned to fly we used to practice dropping bombs—-imaginary ones, of course—-but we were so inaccurate at it that none of us imagined we would be of much use in that direction in actual warfare. I have heard it said that the Germans directed their artillery by signals dropped from aircraft at the very beginning. They did so before they had fought many weeks, anyway. Boche fliers, English gunners have told me, used to hover over battery positions and drop long colored streamers and odd showers of colored lights. It was some time before the Allied airman contributed much to the value of the Allied gunfire. When they got at it, they beat the Huns at their own game, for the war had not been on many months before British planes were flying over Boche batteries and sending back wireless messages from wireless telegraph installations on the machines themselves.

"The Boches had lots more machines than the Allies, and their army command had apparently worked out plans about using them which were new to our side. I saw some of the early war-work of the British fliers, for I got into the Army Service Corps, the transport service, and came out to the front early in 1915. I did not get transferred into the flying part of the business until the end of that year. There is no question but that the quality of the British flying men was what put them ahead of the Germans long before they were equal mechanically. The French, too, are really great fliers. The Boches try hard, and are certainly brave enough, but there is something in the Boche makeup that makes him bound to be second-best to our lot. I have heard lots of discussions on the subject, and I think those who argue that the Boche lacks an element of sportsmanship just about hit the weak point in his armor as regards flying.

"The flying game has been one long succession of discarding the machines we thought best at one time. That applies to the Germans as much as it does to us. One has to go back to the start to realize how much flying has progressed. First, engine construction is another thing to-day. They can make engines in England now, though they were a long time getting to the point where they could do it. I believe that most all the best motor factories in England have learned to turn out good flying engines by now. It means a lot of difference to produce a machine that can do sixty miles an hour and one that can do two miles a minute. Yet at the start mighty few aeroplanes could beat sixty miles an hour, and to-day I can show you plenty of planes right here in this 'drome which can do one hundred and twenty. If a plane cannot do two miles a minute nowadays it is pretty sure to meet something in enemy hands that can do so. Why, before long one hundred and twenty may be too slow.

"Then look at altitudes! When I first thought of flying, five thousand feet up was big. That was not so very long ago. Before the war some very specially built machines, no good for general work, had been coaxed up to about fifteen thousand feet by some crack airman, who had worked for hours to do it, but the best machine we had at the 'drome where I learned flying would only do six thousand, and no one could get her up there under forty minutes. She was a fine machine, too, as machines went in those days. To-day it is no exaggeration to say that ten thousand feet above the earth is low to a flier. Everyone goes to twenty thousand continually, and many of the biggest fights take place from seventeen thousand to twenty thousand feet up.

"The character of the work we have to do has changed as much as the machines have changed. First, anti-aircraft guns—-'Archies,' we call them—- have improved enormously. In the first of the show the airman merely had to keep five thousand feet up and no Archie could touch him. A French friend of mine told me the other day that one of their anti-aircraft guns hit a flier at a height of fifteen thousand feet. The gun was firing from an even greater distance than that across country, too. The very fact that flying at considerable height protected aircraft when scouting produced scientific methods into the collection of information.

"The camera work that has been evolved in this war is little short of wonderful. When it was realized that the planes could get photographs from a height that was out of reach of the Archies of those days, fighting one aeroplane with another came next. Fights in the air, instead of being rare, became the daily routine. I doubt if any of the planes that began the war game in 1914 were armed with rapid-fire guns. The aviators carried automatic pistols or rifles. Some carried ordinary service revolvers.

"With the introduction of the actual air fighting as a part of the scheme of things, three distinct jobs were developed. First, the reconnaissances, which the scouts had to make daily. Next, the artillery observers, whose work it was to direct our gun-fire. Next, the fighters, pure and simple. Another job was bombing, but we have not had as much of that as of the other branches of the work.

"With the coming of the new element—-the fighting planes, which went out with the sole idea of individual combat—-came the necessity for swifter planes, for the man on the fastest machine has the great advantage in the air. The latest development is along the line of team-work in attack. So it goes on changing. I think the smaller, speedier aeroplanes are becoming harder to manage, but we do things now we never dreamed of doing a year ago. All of us can fly now as we never thought before the war it would be possible to fly.

"Instead of rifles and pistols in the hands of the aviators every plane now has at least one rapid-fire gun, and some have two and even three. The position of the rapid-fire gun on an aeroplane has a lot to do with the success or failure of a fight in the air. All of you want to study that question carefully.

"But most fascinating of all to the new airman at the front is the actual handling of the machines when fighting. There lies the greatest progress of all. Construction has made big strides, but fliers have made bigger ones. Wait till you get up front and see."

CHAPTER V

JIMMY HILL STARTLES THE VETERANS

The Brighton boys lived every hour at that big base airdrome. Jimmy Hill was sent up on his first practice flight on an English machine. Joe Little got his chance at the end of a week. He was sent up one morning in a late-type bombing machine, a huge three-seated biplane with great spreading wings and a powerful engine. This was a most formidable looking machine in which one passenger sat out in front mounted in a sort of machine-gun turret. The big biplane was fast, in spite of the heavy armament it carried, its three passengers and its arrangement for carrying hundreds of pounds of bombs as well.

Harry Corwin was in the air at the same time on an artillery machine, the car or fuselage of which projected far in front of the two planes. There, well in front of the pilot, the observer sat in a turret with a machine-gun. Machine-guns were also mounted on the wings, and a second passenger rode in the tail with another rapid-fire gun.

As Bob Haines had been on a rather long flight that day on a Nieuport, a fast French biplane, and his observer had told Bob of a new French dreadnought machine carrying two machine gunners and five machine-guns, the boys talked armament long into the night.

Every day they learned some new points. One afternoon a pilot from the front line told of a captured German Albatros, which he spun yarns about for an hour. A single-seater, armed with three machine-guns which, being controlled by the motor, or engine, shot automatically and at the same time through the propeller in front of the pilot, with the highest speed of any aeroplane then evolved on the fighting front, with a reputation of being able to climb to an altitude of fifteen thousand feet in less than fifteen minutes—some said in so short a time as ten minutes—the crack German machine had attracted much attention.

"With that sort of thing against us," said Dicky Mann, "we have certainly got to learn to fly."

The same thought may have come to their squadron commander that night, for the next day saw the start of real post-graduate work in flying for his command. The rule at the base airdrome had been to give new units of well-trained flyers good all-round tests on various types of machines. This involved straight flying for the most part, and was done more with the idea of familiarizing the newcomers with the newer types of planes, and deciding for which branch of the work they were best suited, than for anything else. In the work that gave the finishing touch to his command, their squadron commander selected three of the six Brighton boys as candidates for high honors in the days to come. Every one of the half dozen was good. All were eager. All flew well. But Joe Little, Jimmy Hill and Harry Corwin seemed made of exactly the sort of stuff from which flying stars were evolved.

"I think I will try to make hunters out of those three boys," said their commander to the officer in charge of the base airdrome.

"Our plan here," said the officer thus addressed, "is to pass youngsters out after they have satisfactorily gone through a final test of two short voyages of twenty-five miles each, two long voyages of one hundred and thirty-five miles each and an hour's flight at a minimum altitude of sixty-five hundred feet. The post-graduate course is mostly aerial acrobatics. Looping the loop comes first. All of them can do that. The flier must then do flip-flops, wing slips, vertical twists and spinning nose dives."

"Just what do you call a spinning nose dive?" asked the squadron commander.

The chief explained: "Climbing to at least four thousand feet, the pilot cuts off his motor and crosses his controls. This causes the machine first to scoop upward and then fall sidewise, the nose of the plane, down vertically, spinning around and around as it falls."

"That sounds interesting," said the commander.

"More," continued the chief. "It is necessary. Skill in the air nowadays means all the difference between life and death—-all the difference between success and defeat. I have an idea that we have come nearer to the limit of human possibility as regards speed in the air than many people think. Two hundred miles an hour may never be reached. But whether it is or not, we can get better and better results by paying more and more attention to the development of our aerial athletes.

"I look on flyers as athletes playing a game—-the greatest game the world has ever seen. The more expert we can make them individually, the better the service will be. A nimble flyer, a real star man, is almost sure to score off a less expert antagonist, even if the better man is mounted on an inferior plane. That has been proven to me beyond all possibility of doubt time and time again.

"I was once a football coach. My work here, so far as it touches men, is very similar to coaching work. It comes down to picking the good ones, sorting them out, weeding, weeding all the time. You like those particular three boys you referred to? Well, watch them. Give them chances. But don't be disappointed if they are not all world-beaters. And don't be surprised if some of the lot you think will stick at the steadier, plainer work turn out big. You never can tell."

Before the strain of expert acrobatics came careful training in machine-gunnery. The Brighton boys went through a course of study on land that made them thoroughly familiar with machine-guns of more than one type. Machine-guns, they found, were in all sorts of positions on the different sorts of machines.

"I wonder where they will put a rapid-fire gun next?" said Joe Little one day at luncheon. "Let's see. I saw one plane this morning that had a gun mounted on the upper plane, and fired above the propeller. Another next to it had the gun placed in the usual position in front, and fired through the propeller. Next I ran across a movable gun on a rotating base fixed at the rear of the supporting planes. Of course all of those big triple planes have the fuselage mounting, and I was surprised to see still another sort of mounting, a movable gun fixed behind the keel of one of those new English 'pushers,' just as I came in. It keeps a fellow busy to see all the new things here, and no mistake."

"Your talk is so much Greek to me sometimes, Joe," said Bob Haines. "You use so much technical language when you get going that you fog me. I can make a plane do what it is supposed to do, most of the time, but some of these special ideas floor me, and I am not ashamed to admit it."

"What is worrying you specially?" asked Jimmy Hill, smiling.

Bob was one of the soundest fliers of the six of them, but he was forever making hard work out of anything he did not understand from the ground up. Once he had mastered the why and wherefore, he was at peace, but if the reason was hidden from him he was never quite sure on that point.

"It is this," answered Bob. "Most all of the machines they have been putting me up against lately have been those speedy little one-man things—-the hunters. Now I understand all about the necessity for speed and agility in that type, and I can see that the fixed gun in front, sticking out like a finger in such fashion that you have to point the plane at a Boche to point the gun at him, is a thing they can't well get away from. That Hartford type of hunter just over from home is rigged up that way, and I can get the little gun on her pointed anyway I like. But all guns fixed that way fire through the propeller, and just exactly how all those bullets manage to get through those whirring blades without hitting one of them is not quite clear to me yet."

"Go it, Joe," said Harry Corwin. "You spent a good time listening to what that French pilot said about Garros the other day."

"The Frenchman told me that a very well known pilot of the early days of the war, named Garros, invented the arrangement whereby a gun could be so mounted that the bullets went through the arc of the revolving propeller blades," answered Joe. "He said, too, that Garros had the bad luck to be taken prisoner, and the Germans got his machine before he had any chance to destroy it. That was the way the Germans got hold of the idea. Garros simply designed a bit of mechanism that automatically stops the gun from firing when the propeller blade is passing directly in front of the gun-barrel. He placed the gun-barrel directly behind the propeller. He then made a cam device so regulated as to fire the gun with a delay not exceeding one five-hundredth of a second. As soon as the blade of the propeller passes the barrel the system liberates the firing mechanism of the gun until another blade passes, or is about to pass, when the bullets that would pierce it are held up, just for that fraction of a second, again. So it goes on, like clockwork. You have noticed that on the new planes all the pilot has to do when he wants to fire his machine-gun is to press a small lever which is set, on most planes, in the handle of the directing lever. That small lever acts, by the mechanism I have told you about, on the trigger of the gun. It is simple enough."

"Yes," admitted Bob, "it does not sound very complicated, but it seems very wonderful, all the same. Most things out here are wonderful when you first run into them, though."

Of the group of Brighton boys selected by the squadron commander to study the finer points of aerial acrobatics, Joe Little was the star, with Harry Corwin a very close second and Jimmy Hill a good third. Their education, as the days went past, became a series of experiments that were nothing short of hair-raising to any onlookers save most experienced ones.

To see Joe, in a wasp of a plane, swift and agile, start it whirling like a pinwheel with the tip of its own wing as an axis, and fall for thousands of feet as it whirled, only to catch himself and right the speedy plane when lees than a thousand feet from the earth, was indeed a sight to make one hold one's breath.

Jimmy Hill learned a dodge that interested older aviators. Looping the loop sidewise, he would catch the plane when upside down, and shoot away at a tangent, head down, the machine absolutely inverted—-then continue the side loop, bringing him back to upright again some distance from where he had originally begun his evolution.

Watching him at this stunt, a veteran pilot said to the chief one morning: "That turn will save that kid's life one day. See if it don't." And sure enough, one day, it did.

Harry learned what a French friend had told him the great Guynemer, king of all French fliers, had christened "the dead leaf." With the plane bottom side up, the pilot lets it fall, now whirling downward, now seeming to hang for a moment, suspended in midair, now caught by an eddy and tossed upward, just like a dead leaf is tossed by an autumn wind.

Joe could nose-dive to perfection. He would hover high up, at well over ten thousand feet from the ground, then drop straight for the earth, like a plummet, nose directly downward, seemingly bent on destruction. When still at a safe distance up, he would gradually ease his rush through the air by "teasing her a bit," as he called it. Then, before the eye from below could follow his evolutions, he would be skimming off on a level course like a swallow.

The day came at last when the squadron was "moved up front" for actual work over the enemy's lines. The Brighton boys were ready and eager to give a good account of themselves, and soon they were to be accorded ample opportunity.

CHAPTER VI

The morning on which the Brighton boys left the base airdrome with their squadron saw the first sunshine that that part of France had known for several days. The line of light motor trucks which served as their transport skimmed along the long, straight roads as if aware that they carried the cavalry of the air.

"France is a pretty country. I had no idea it would look so much like home. Those fields and the hills beyond might be right back where we come from, boys," said Archie Fox.

"Wait till you youngsters get up a bit," advised a companion who had seen the front line often before. "You will see a part of France that won't remind you of anything you have ever seen!"

In spite of that mention of the horrors that they all knew war had brought in its train, it was hard to imagine them while swinging along at a good pace through countryside that looked so quiet and peaceful. The line of lorries slowed down for a level crossing, where the road led across a spur of railway, and then halted, the gate-keeper having blocked the highway to allow the passing of a still distant and very slowly moving train. The gate-keeper was a buxom and determined-looking French woman of well past middle age, who turned a deaf ear to the entreaties of the occupants of the leading car that the line of trucks should be allowed to scurry across before the train passed.

As the boys sat waiting in the sudden quiet, Picky Mann said quietly:

"We are getting nearer. Listen to the guns."

Sure enough, their attention drawn to the distant growling, the dull booming of the detonations of the high-explosive shells could be distinctly heard. War was ahead, at last, and not so very far ahead at that. Not long after, the squadron passed through a shattered French village.

Every one of the boys had seen pictures in plenty of shell-smashed ruins, but the actuality of the awful devastation made them hold their breath for a moment. To think that such desolate piles of brick and mortar were once rows of human habitations, peopled with men, women and children very much like the men, women and children in their own land, sobered the boys.

Soon Bob Haines drew the attention of the others to captive balloons along the sky-line ahead, and finally the Brighton boys saw a black smudge in the air far in front. It was a minute or two before they realized that they had seen their first bursting shell.

The leading car turned sharply off the highway into a by-road at right angles to it. A hundred yards further it dashed through a gap in a tall hedge, and as the line of trucks followed it, they emerged upon a great flying field.

There, ahead, were still the captive balloons, straining at their leashes probably, but too far away to show anything but the general outline of their odd sausage shapes. Ahead, too, was the boom of the guns. No mistaking that. Their aeroplanes were to be the eyes of those very guns. They knew that well. The front line was up there, somewhere. Their own soldiers, their comrades, were in that line. Perhaps some of them were being shelled by the Boche guns at that very moment.

"Beyond our lines," they thought, "come the enemy lines. Soon, now, very soon, some of us will be flying over those lines, and far back of them, perhaps."

To the credit of the Brighton boys, every one of the six of them felt a real keenness to get to work and take his part in the great game. They had waited long and worked hard to perfect themselves for the tasks that lay ahead of them, up there with the guns and beyond. There was no feeling of shrinking from the awful reality of actual war, now that it came nearer and nearer to them. They were of sound stuff, to a man.

The wooden huts that were to be their homes for a time were clean and dry, and the big barn-like hangars that stood near had a serviceable look about them. The level field that stretched away in front of the hangars was dotted here and there with a dozen planes, couples of men, or small groups, working on each one. Before they realized it they were a part of the camp.

Immediately after dinner the flight commander sent for them and provided each of them with a set of maps. All the next morning they pored over these, consulting the wonderfully complete set of photographs of the enemy country which could be found in the photograph department of the airdrome.

Practice flights took up the afternoon, and Joe Little and Jimmy Hill tried to outmaneuver one another at fairly high altitudes.

More than once Joe managed to get his machine-gun trained direct on Jimmy, but finally Jimmy side-looped with extraordinary cleverness, dashed off and up while still inverted, then righted suddenly and found himself "right on the tail" of Joe's machine, i.e., behind Joe and above him, in the best possible position for aeroplane attack. Joe had looped after a short nose-dive, hoping Jimmy would be below him when he pulled up, but the odd inverted swing upward that was Jimmy's star turn had found him in the better position when the duel ended.

As the boys landed the flight commander walked toward them. They stepped from their machines and came in his direction, laughingly discussing their mimic battle. As the flight commander drew near, he beckoned to them.

"Do you do that regularly?" he asked Jimmy.

"Yes, sir," was Jimmy's reply.

"Has it ever appeared to damage your planes?"

"No, sir. Not that I am aware."

That was all. Just a casual question from the chief. But it made

Jimmy feel that he was not so much of a novice as he had felt before.

He felt that he was more "part of the show," as he would have put it

if he had been asked to describe his feelings.

Jimmy was the first of the Brighton boys to take part in a real fight in the air. A couple of days after his arrival at the airdrome he was assigned to duty with an experienced aviator named Parker. Both Parker and Jimmy were to be mounted on fast, agile machines with very little wing space, which, with their slightly-curved, fish-like bodies, had the appearance of dragon-flies with short wings.

"These wasp-things are great for looping," said Parker to Jimmy. "You can throw them 'way over in a big arc that lands you a long distance from where some of these Boche fliers expect you to be when you finish your loop."

"What is the game we are to tackle?" asked Jimmy.

"Just hunting, I think. The Boches seem to have become a little bolder than usual during the last forty-eight hours. Two of their observation planes came unusually close to us yesterday. I suppose they may have received orders to spot something they can't find, and it is worrying them a bit. I guess the chief is going to send us out together to see if we can bag one of their scout planes. Their hunters will be guarding. It is better to go out in twos, if not in lots, along this part of the line. As a matter of fact, it is more than likely that some German on a new Fokker or a Walvert is sitting up aloft there like a sweet little cherub and laying for us. They have a nasty habit of swooping down like a hawk when we get well over their territory and firing as they swoop. If they get you, you drop in their part of the country. If they miss you, they just swing off and forget it, or climb back and sit on the mat till another of our lot comes along. Swooping and missing don't put them in much danger, for if they come down they are in their own area."

"Have you had one of them try that hawk game on you?" asked Jimmy.

"I have had the pleasure and honor to have the great Immelmann drop at me, once, on an Albatros, or a machine that looked like an Albatros. We knew afterward that it was Immelmann, for he worked the same tactics several times, always in the same way. I was out guarding one of our fellows who was getting pictures pretty well back of the Boche lines, when along came a regular fleet of German aircraft.

"Four of them took after me, and I had to think quick. I couldn't skip exactly, for I had to give the observation bus a chance to get a start. I maneuvered into a pretty good position, under the circumstances, and was going to fire a round into them and then dive for home and mother, when the bullets began to sing about me from a fifth plane. I couldn't see it, so I flip-flopped chop-chop. As I turned I saw Immelmann's plane swoop past. I turned over just in the nick of time and he missed me, though his nasty gun-fire pretty well chewed up my bottom plane.

"I did a hurried dead-leaf act, and I guess the Germans thought I was done for and dropping, for they lit out without bothering any more about me. I got home without any further incident, and found the observation fellow had got back without a scratch, and had managed to just finish his job before we were attacked, which was lucky."

Jimmy had taken in every syllable of Parker's story. He had tried to picture himself in the same bad fix, and had caught the idea of Parker's lightning action. "This fellow must be as quick as a cat," he thought. "I wonder if I would have had sense enough to grasp the situation in the way he did? Well, if I get in a similar fix I will have some idea of what to do, thanks to him."

Weeks afterward Jimmy heard that story of Parker's fight with five Boche planes from another source. He then learned that Parker had omitted an interesting feature of the tale. Before Immelmann swooped on him, Parker had smashed up and sent to ground two of the four Boche machines which had originally attacked him.

The Brighton boys soon learned that the most outstanding characteristic of veteran fliers was modesty. A new chivalry had sprung up with the development of the air service. Every successful flier had to be a thorough sportsman to win through, and never did the boys meet a real veteran at the, game who would tell of his own successes.

The general view of the flying men at the front was that the man who did the prosaic work of daily reconnaissance and got back safe and sound, without frequent spectacular combats and hair-breadth escapes that made good telling, was just as much of a hero and took his life in his hands just as surely, as did the man who went out to individual duel with an adversary, and accomplished some stunt that had a spice of novelty in it.

The second in command at the airdrome gave Parker and Jimmy their final instructions. "This is Hill's first time over," said the officer to Parker. "He can fly, though. I think for the first time he had better guard and watch." Then, turning to Jimmy: "Watch Parker, and fly about eight hundred feet behind him and the same distance above him when he straightens out. Parker will attack when he sees a Boche. Your job will still be to sit tight and watch until you can see how things are going. A second Boche or maybe more than one other will be pretty sure to show up, and it will be your job to attack whatever comes along and drive it off so that it can't interfere with Parker while he is finishing off his man.

"If anything should happen to Parker, be sure what you take on before you go after the plane he first tackled, for usually you will find more than one plane about over there on their side. Don't forget one thing. If you find that you are surrounded run for it. That machine you are to fly will give them a chase, no matter how they are mounted. Remember, we haven't many of those, yet, and cannot afford to lose any." As he said this, the officer laughed.

Jimmy felt he should have smiled, too, but his head was too full of his job. He said "Yes, sir," quite seriously, and turned to give his machine a final tuning up.

Jimmy jumped into the driving seat with a very determined feeling. He must give a good account of himself, come what might. He fixed his head-gear a bit tighter, pulled on his gloves, and tried the position of his machine-gun. There it sat, just above the hood, a bit to the right, almost in front of Jimmy. He felt a sudden affection for it. How it would make some Boche sit up if he came into range!

The wheels were blocked with shaped pieces of wood, and Jimmy nodded to his mechanics to start the engine. One whirl of the shining blades, and the engine started, to roar away in deafening exuberance of power as it warmed to its work. Something was not quite right. The rhythm was not just perfect. Jimmy stopped the engine, ordered a plug changed, and then, the order executed in a jiffy, nodded to his men to once more start the motor. This time the engine droned out a perfect series of explosions.

The flight sub-commander stepped beside the fuselage as Jimmy shut off the engine, and said: "I have given detailed instructions to Parker. You are to watch him and stay with him. If you by any chance lose him, come back. Are your maps and instruments all right?"

"Yes, sir."

Then off with you, and good luck. You will be doing this sort of thing every day before long, but I expect it seems a bit new to you at first."

"Yes, sir. Thank you, sir."

A final nod to his men—-the roar once more, louder, more vibrant, more defiant than ever—-a quick signal of the hand, and the cords attached to the blocks under the wheels were given a jerk. Jimmy was off on his dangerous mission!

Old force of habit, a relic of earlier days of aeronautics, sent the men to the wings, where they gave the big dragon-fly an unnecessary push. After a run of a few feet Jimmy raised her suddenly, swiftly, and she darted up almost perpendicularly. He realized as never before that he was mounted on a machine that could probably outclimb and outtrick any antagonist he was likely to meet.

"This is sure some bus," he thought to himself. "I guess she will do all that is asked of her, whatever she runs into. So it's up to me. If I fly her right she will come home, sure."

As he climbed into the clear sky he could see Parker's machine ahead, circling higher and higher. He was glad Parker was going, too. There was an odd but unmistakable sense of companionship in having Parker up there ahead, though at fifteen thousand feet up or more, and at eight hundred to a thousand feet distant, it seemed silly to think of a man as "near" in case of trouble. Beside, he was to guard Parker, and no one was to guard him.

But the powerful hunter on which he was mounted thrilled with such a feeling of self-satisfaction, her engines hummed so merrily, and she lifted herself so lightly and easily when he asked her to climb, that he was soon wrapped in the joy of mastering so perfect a piece of mechanism. Moreover, Jimmy had grown to love flying for flying's sake. It was meat and drink to him.

When Parker had gained the altitude that suited him he straightened out and headed for the enemy's country at a high rate of speed. Jimmy thought himself too far behind at first, but the splendid machine answered readily to his call upon it for a burst of five minutes, and before he had time to realize it he was in good position and far below were the long, winding scars on the surface of the earth that told where the opposing armies were entrenched. Fighting the temptation to watch what was passing underneath, he alternately kept his eyes on Parker and scoured the sky ahead for signs of enemy aircraft.

Suddenly, between Parker and his own machine, and not so far below him as he would have liked, white puff-balls began to appear. The German anti-aircraft guns were at it. Parker began a wide sweep to the left, then turned slowly right, then climbed swiftly. Jimmy raised his machine at the same time, but, thinking to save the left turn and unconsciously slowing in a little on the plane in front, was reminded that he would be wise to change course a bit. The ominous whirr of pieces of projectile told him that the German "Archie" had fired a shot with good direction. He knew that shell might be closely followed by another at a better elevation, so turned right, climbing, until he had regained his eight hundred feet or more above Parker.

As he did so Parker circled left once more, then flew at right angles to the course he had originally selected. No more shells came near; and again Parker changed course.

As Jimmy was trying to surmise where Parker would head next the swift wasp in front dived suddenly, as if struck by one of the anti-aircraft projectiles.

Quickly Jimmy dived also, and as he turned the nose of the machine downward his heart gave a big bound, for right in front of Parker, some distance below, was the wide wing-spread of a big German machine. The enemy plane could hardly see Parker, save by some miracle, before he had come sufficiently near to pour a murderous fire into it. With a rush, his instructions came back to him. He must hover above and watch, whatever the result of the combat below him. He straightened out, and circling narrowly, scanned the air in every direction. As he swung round he received another shock, a real one this time.

Straight before him, plainly coming as fast as they could fly, were three planes of a type unfamiliar to him. They were at about his own altitude. He called on his machine for all she could produce in the way of power, and depressed his elevator planes. The moment the nose of his plane turned upward, the three enemy planes began to climb also. Jimmy dared not try a steeper angle of ascent. Any machine which he had ever seen, save his new mount, would have refused to climb as she was doing.

What should he do? For the moment he could not see the fight below him between Parker and the plane Parker had started to chase. Surely, with three to one against him, the best thing he could do would be to keep his own skin intact. Intuitively glancing upward, what was his horror to see, still high up but dropping like a meteor, a fourth enemy plane—-a big Gotha! It came over him like a flash! The Boches were at their game. While the three lower planes engaged his attention, a watcher had sat aloft. The German plan, Parker had told him, was to swoop down from a great height and catch the unwary Allied flier unawares.

Stopping his engine, he side-slipped out of the path of the newcomer, rolled over once or twice to befog the enemy as to his intentions, and then sailed aside still further on one of his "upside-down stunts," which had caught the eye of the flight commander. He thus escaped the swoop of the diving Gotha, and as the other three Germans turned to the right to demolish him, he swung half round, righted himself, and climbed for dear life. In very few minutes he was above them, leading the chase, all three pressing after him, and spreading out fan-wise slightly to ensure catching him if he again tried the maneuver that had extricated him from the former trap.

For a few moments Jimmy felt a mite nervous as to how things were coming out. Then it dawned on him that he was doing his part well if he drew the enemy fighters after him and away from Parker. The fourth of the Boche hunters might be after him still, back there behind him, or it might be fighting Parker, wherever Parker might be. By a quick glance back he could see the three pursuers. Their planes, too, were climbing well. He straightened out to try a burst of level speed. Examining his map and compass he saw he was not heading for home. That was bad. He tried veering to the left a bit, but imagined that the plane behind him on the left drew nearer.

Then Jimmy found himself. What was it Parker had said about the new hunter-machines being splendid loopers? Why not try a loop? Would the Boches get wise to the idea quickly? Perhaps not quickly enough. If he did a big, fast loop, he might come right-side-up on the tail of one or even two of his would-be destroyers, and if he could only get that wicked little rapid-firer of his to bear he would lessen the odds against him, of that he felt sure. In a very few seconds after the idea had come to him he had decided to put it into practice.

The big wasp turned a beautiful arc, swiftly, neatly, as if it had known the game and was eager to take part in it. No machine could have performed a more perfect loop; and, as he had hoped, it brought him in the rear of the group of assailants. The center one of the three enemy planes was nearest to him. Straight at it Jimmy dashed, and when close, started firing. It was the first time in his life that Jimmy had tried to take a human life, but he did not give that fact a thought. A fierce desire to finish off the flier so close in front overwhelmed him. He felt that he could not miss. A second or two passed after the burst of fire before any change in the conduct of the plane in front was noticeable.

Then the change came; all at once. The machine turned on its side, the engine still running at full speed, and for one instant, before the downward plunge came, Jimmy caught sight of a limp, lifeless form half-hanging, sidewise, from the pilot's seat. Jimmy had fired straight, and one of his antagonists was out of the fight.

He turned his attention to the flier on his left, fired a round at him at rather long range, and then glanced to his right. It was well he did so at that instant. The German on the right of the trio had looped in turn, to get on to Jimmy's tail. Jimmy saw the trick in the nick of time, and letting the left-hand plane go for the moment, looped in turn. As he turned, he saw what he thought must be the fourth enemy machine—-the big fellow that had swooped down on him at the beginning of the fight—-speeding straight at him. He quickly turned his loop into a side-loop, slid down swiftly, caught himself, and assured that he had escaped both fliers for the moment, took a rapid glance at his compass and saw that he was headed straight for home. And home Jimmy went, as fast as his machine would go.

CHAPTER VII

PARKER'S STORY

This time he had a very fair start, and he made the best of it. Looking back, he saw that two of the German machines headed after him, but apparently gave up the chase before it was well begun. Once Jimmy had a feeling that he ought not to run back to safety before endeavoring, to see what had happened to Parker, but the flight sub-commander had been most explicit in his instructions on that head. "If you by any chance lose Parker," he had said, "come back." He had lost Parker, right enough. That was about the first thing he had done, he thought to himself with some feeling of self-condemnation.

All the while he was roaring on, his machine seemingly feeling like a homing pigeon. He felt a fierce love for that noble hunter. He felt he could almost talk to it and tell it how proud he was of having been able to put it through its paces. Never had there been such a machine before, he thought.

At last the home airdrome came into sight far below. Many a time thereafter was Jimmy to feel glad he was nearing home, but never more sincerely than on the afternoon of that first battle. He made a good landing. His mechanics were waiting for him, and wheeled the machine toward the hangar, while Jimmy walked off to headquarters to report. Arrived there, he found that both the flight commander and sub-commander were out. No one seemed worrying much about him. He had been so intent on his job and it had meant so much to him that it took a few minutes for him to get the right perspective, and see that, after all, he was only one of the pieces in the big game, and a bit of waiting would not hurt him or make his report any the less of interest.

Would it be of interest? The thought came to him as he sat there, quietly. What would he report? The flight commander was a busy person. He would not, in all probability, have the time to hear a long report, should he have the inclination to do so. What could Jimmy report? First that he had lost Parker. Where in the name of goodness was Parker? Jimmy would have given much to know, but something kept him from asking. He had been sent out as a sort of guard for Parker. He had lost him at the very beginning of the fight. He might report that he had shot down an enemy hunter machine and killed its pilot, but surely that would sound very bare and very boastful.

Just as Jimmy was really making himself thoroughly miserable the door of the rough headquarters shed opened, and who should walk in but Parker himself! Jimmy felt he could have hugged him.

"I was sitting here wondering where you were," said Jimmy.

"Well, for the most part I have been chasing you," answered the older pilot. "You certainly can fly that machine you were on to-day, young fellow! If I were you I would ask the chief to let you stick to that plane. You put up a swell little exhibition in her to-day."

"Chasing me?" Jimmy gasped. "Chasing me? I don't understand."

"It is simple enough. I suppose you saw me go for that big dray-horse of a scout machine, didn't you?"

Jimmy nodded.

"I got him, I think," Parker went on. "Anyway, he went down. He seemed to land pretty well, for a smash, but that sort of plane will almost land by itself, sometimes. When I was sure he was down, sure enough, I had come a bit too low, and for a while I was pretty busy dodging the finest collection of Archies I have yet met with. I got two fair-sized pieces of shell right through both planes, but they didn't seem to matter a bit. I got up to a good height before I quit climbing. So far as I could see, you had by that time managed to get out of what must have been a bit of a trap, and were heading off south at a rate of knots, as my sailor brother would say. I hovered, watching the big hunter that dived on you. He didn't seem to know quite what to do. He must have missed seeing me, for some reason.

"As I was waiting for him to make up his mind you did that ripping loop. I saw that. So did the Boche hunter who was onlooking. I knew you would get that center plane, and thought you would score two of them, but you were right to take no chances of the number three chap getting a drop on you. Where I played the goat was letting the swooper fellow get a start on me. I guess I was too interested watching your antics."

"Anyway, he got to your area before I did, though I wasn't far back. Your skid off to the side put them all off, and gave me a fine chance at Mr. Swooper. He fussed a minute, undecided what to do. That is a bad fault at this game. I caught him just where I wanted him, and he did his last swoop, I guess. I piled on home after you, but not so fast. Anyone would think you were going to a fire, by the way you came back. What was your desperate hurry?"

Jimmy laughed. He was so glad Parker was home safe and sound that he did not mind being chaffed. So Parker had accounted for two enemy machines? And he had been worrying about Parker! Well, he might as well own up to himself, he thought, that he had been acting like a very green hand at the game. But never mind! They had done a good day's work, both of them. No mistake about that. He felt good. The reaction had set in in earnest. Jimmy was simply happy.

At that moment the flight commander came in. Parker and Jimmy rose, stepped forward and saluted.

"Back?" said the chief laconically.

"Yes, sir," answered Parker.

"Did you find any of their scouts?"

"Yes, sir. One."

"Get him?"

"Drove him down, sir. I could not tell much about his damage from his landing, though I think he smashed a bit. I had a good chance at him."

"That all?"

"Yes, sir. Except that four of their hunters attacked Hill. He side-looped and got free, then looped again and caught one well, finishing him. He threw one other right into my hands, too."

"Get him?"

"Yes, sir."

"Right." The flight commander turned to go out, then, as if suddenly remembering that Jimmy was a new hand at the game, he said over his shoulder: "Very well done. Get Parker to show you how to make out your report. Very good, both of you."

"H'm," said Parker as the chief stepped out of the door. "He is getting talkative."

But the flight commander was more voluble when he saw Jimmy's squadron commander that night. "I think that youngster you brought up with you—boy by the name of Hill—is made of good stuff," he said. "He went with Parker to-day, and between them they managed a very pretty show. I shall read their official reports with interest. It isn't very often a young fellow gets such a baptism, and it's still more rare for one to pull it off the way Hill did. Why, those two got two, if not three Boches. Think of it! If Hill keeps on the way he has started out he will make a name for himself."

"I picked him as a possible good one," said the squadron commander proudly. "I think he will keep it up."

Jimmy, though tired, did not go to sleep the minute he went to bed that night. He lay for ten or fifteen minutes going over what the day had brought him. Curiously enough, the last thing he said to himself, before he dropped off to sleep, was very much akin to what his squadron leader had said.

CHAPTER VIII

THRILLS OF THE UPPER REACHES

To the great delight of the Brighton boys, Will Corwin paid a visit to them one evening, and stayed to dinner at their mess. Will was not much older than his brother Harry, so far as years went, but he looked ten years older. The constant work on the French front had bronzed him and made him leaner and harder than when he left his home in America.

He had many questions to ask the boys about the home folks, and said that he had been trying to get a chance to visit Harry for weeks. Will was particularly interested to hear what had been the experiences of the Brighton fliers in connection with their first real work at the front.

Four of the boys had been over the German lines by that time. Like Jimmy Hill, Joe Little had been out on a hunter machine. His experiences were uneventful, however. His job had been to watch, with another hunter, while a speedy, big bomber dropped hundreds of pounds of explosives on an enemy munition dump.

The whole affair went through like a dress rehearsal, and without a hitch. They flew straight for their objective, found it without the slightest difficulty, deposited a load of high explosives upon it in quick time, and soared away back home without a single encounter with an enemy plane. They were, it was true, severely "Archied," as they called it, but no one of them was the worse for it.

Harry Corwin had been over the Boche lines three times, and had found the experience quite sufficiently exciting, though he had not been in actual combat at close quarters with the enemy as had Jimmy Hill.

His work for three mornings had been to escort a certain observation plane which had been sent each day to watch the development of a reserve line of dugouts well in the rear of the German front line. As a matter of fact, the pilot of the observation machine, a swift triplane, was well known as a dead shot. He needed an escort machine less than Harry did, Harry thought.

That triplane was about as formidable in appearance as any aircraft could be. It was only a two-seater, but it was armed with two machine-guns, singularly well placed. The front rapid-firer was fixed between the two supporting planes, the barrel next to the motor and parallel with it. This front gun was fired by Richardson, the pilot of the triplane, who controlled it with his right hand. This was a radical departure from some of the more usual gun positions, in which the gun was customarily located on the upper plane and operated by the observer.

Having a gun all to himself had pleased Richardson mightily, and he had become a wonderful shot.

The second gun on the triplane was placed on the framework behind the observer's station. It was mounted on a revolving base, and had an exceptionally wide range of fire.

"It is a pure joy, sometimes," Richardson was once heard to say, "to see the way the little major grins when some chesty Boche has thought he had us sure, and comes creeping up behind, only to get a dose right in the nose. That gun of the major's carries further than anything we have run against yet, and he just couldn't miss a Hun to save his life." The major was Richardson's observer.

Another yarn that Richardson was accustomed to tell on his companion of the upper reaches ran as follows: "When they first put me at carting observation planes around I was pretty green. I had but very shortly before done my first solo in England. The British were fairly short of fliers then, or I should not have been sent out. I arrived at the airdrome full of conceit, thinking I was a real pilot.

"The morning after I got there they led me out and stood me alongside a double-seater. The boss of that shop told me he wanted to see me take it around for a try-out, and then it was off and away for the front. He said considerately that I might wait a few minutes until another new arrival had done his little preliminary canter.

"The other victim started up, taxied toward the other side of the field that served for an airdrome, and lifted too late, with the result that he caught the wheels of his chassis in the tall hedge and came down in mighty nasty fashion on the other side, just out of sight. That is, he was out of sight. The tail of his plane stuck up to show what a real header he had taken. I found out later that he got out of that smash with a broken leg and a bad shake-up, but when I was standing there by that machine, waiting to go up, I thought the poor devil who had the tumble must have been killed, sure.

"Then up came the major. He was a captain then. He was going to get into his seat when the boss-man said to him: 'I suggest that you wait until he has done a round or so alone.'"

"The little captain snorted at this, but the boss evidently thought it best, so up I went, alone.

"I did well enough, and after feeling the machine thoroughly, came down, making a fine landing. But fate was out with her ax that morning. No one had said a word to me about a ditch that had been dug on the left side of the field, and, of course, I had to find it. When I saw it, no time was left to avoid it, so in I went. Over toppled the poor plane, and smash went my under-works. In fact, I came out of my seat rather quickly, but wasn't really hurt. The boss chap was a bit mad, but the little captain man just laughed.

"Good thing I waited till he had had his little fun," he chuckled. "now we can off and do our work, I suppose."

"I thought he was joking, but he wasn't. He did not mind my smash a bit. I saw that. He went right on up with me in another machine ten minutes later just as though we had been going up together for years. That is the kind of nerve my major has."

Richardson did not realize how very much cool action of the observation officer had to do with the implanting in the pilot of a good sound confidence in himself. Had Richardson but known it, the captain, as he was then, had never been more apprehensive of trouble. He did not like to trust himself to green fliers, any more than another man would have done. But he knew that quick, sure show of confidence was the only thing that would put confidence into Richardson in turn. Such moments are sometimes the crucial ones. At such times fliers may be made or marred in a manner that may be, for good or for ill, irrevocable.

Sent to watch and assist this pair of doughty warriors, Harry Corwin found most of his time in the air spent in keeping in the position which had been assigned to him. Archies were everyday things to Richardson and his major. They did not by any means scorn them, the anti-aircraft guns, as continual improvement was noticeable, not only in their marksmanship, but in their range. But Richardson was a pastmaster at judging when he was well out of range, and equally clever at getting into such a position.

Once Harry had seen a fascinating duel between Richardson and a Boche plane, in which the latter retired before a decision was reached. Once the two American pilots had been compelled to run from a squadron of hunters, who gave up the chase as soon as they drew near to the Allied territory. But Jimmy Hill's exploit, and the fact that he had not only been the hero of a fight against big odds, but had actually brought down a flier and smashed up a hunter machine, loomed so large with the Brighton boys that the more ordinary experiences of the others paled into insignificance in their eyes.

Bob Haines had been on a photographing trip, and had earned great commendation from the observation officer whom he carried. Bob had taken keenly to the scientific work of trench photography, and spent his spare hours in the photographic workshop, which was a storehouse of wonders to him. He was fast getting sound ideas on subjects in connection with air-pictures, which made him all the more valuable as a pilot of a machine that carried some officer of the photographic department.

He had witnessed a very pretty fight between an American and a Boche not far distant, but he could not take part. His observer was a good hand with a Lewis gun, too. They had on board at that time, however, a set of negatives that were of considerable value, which they had been sent specially to obtain, so their duty was to leave the hunter to fare as best he could, while they scurried home in safety with their negatives.

Thus Will Corwin found that the Brighton boys were fast becoming broken in to practical flying work. Archie Fox had been as busy as any of the rest, tuning up a new machine that had a hidden kink in its anatomy somewhere that defied detection.

Dicky Mann had been selected by the flight commander to work up a special set of maps—-office work that required great care. He had been absorbed day and night, and had cut down his sleeping hours to five or six hours instead of the eight or nine he used to indulge in at Brighton.

It was not so exciting as flying, the commander had told him when

he was selected for the job, "but of equal, if not greater, importance."

At all events, Dicky was at it, heart and soul, and the evening that

Will Corwin made his appearance was the first for some days that

Dicky had joined his messmates for a chat after dinner.

"How do you think we Yanks are making out against the Teutons in the air, Will?" asked Harry. "Do you think they are beginning to recognize that we have 'em beaten?"

Will Corwin grinned. "'Beginning to' is good, but that's along way from the finished realization, and I don't guess that will come for some little time yet. It's up to America and the Allies to keep on turning out planes and fliers at top speed."

"What about the wonderful speed of the German machines, Will?" asked

Joe Little.

"An awful lot of rot is talked about speed, as you boys must know. We captured a very decent German flier once, who got lost in a fog and ran out of petrol. When he had to come down he found he was right near our airdrome, so he volplaned right down on our field. We were surprised to see him. He was in an Albatros of a late type, too. As you can imagine, we gave him a very hearty greeting. He took it pretty well, considering everything. I had him into my shack for lunch, and we got quite friendly before they took him back to the base. I remember at that time that the usual talk about Boche flying machines on this front would lead you to believe that they were much faster than we were. At home you could hear almost any speed attributed to the German aeroplanes. I think some Americans thought they could do about two miles to the English or French planes' one.

"I was particularly interested in the Fokkers, Walverts and L.V.G. machines, which were the ones we had to fight most. Now, according to that candid young German, who seemed ready enough to talk frankly about things, anyone of those three planes that did one hundred miles an hour at an elevation of ten thousand feet was considered a mighty good plane. If it did one hundred and twenty miles at that elevation it was thought to be a hummer. They were fast climbers for their speed, and usually did most of their fighting, if they had a choice, at thirteen to fourteen thousand feet up. Only the Albatros could be depended upon to beat one hundred and twenty miles an hour regularly. He said he would rather not tell me the speed of the Albatros, I did not press him. The point of all this is that those very machines he was discussing were credited with speeds of anything up to one hundred and thirty-five or one hundred and fifty miles per hour by lots of people who thought they knew all about it. There will never come a day, in our generation, when one hundred and fifty miles an hour at ten thousand feet up will not be mighty good flying."

"You have been at this game some time now, Will," said Joe Little. "Can you think of anything we ought to specially learn that we won't get hold of in plain flying? A tip is often worth a lot, you know."

"From what I hear from you boys, I guess what Joe means by plain flying means pretty well every sort of stunt. I don't think one fellow can tell another much about that sort of thing. Some of it comes natural and some of it has to be learned by experience. I think fliers are born, not made, anyway. There is one thing you might get some tips upon. That relates to cloud formations. You can't know too much about that. I am expecting a book from home on that subject shortly, and when I wade through it I will let you boys have it."

"The state of the atmosphere plays a bigger part in aerial battles than one might think. Calm days, without the least wind, when the sky is covered by large gray clouds, are, as you all probably know, very favorable for surprise attacks. The clouds act as a screen and allow the aviator to hide himself until the very moment he thinks he can drop on his enemy and take him by surprise.

"The Germans have a scheme they worked pretty successfully for a while. When the clouds lie low, one of their machines dashes around below the clouds, only two or three hundred yards up, and in the area into which the Allied planes are likely to come. This sole machine acts, if the scheme works, as a sort of bait. Sometimes they pick a slow machine of an old model for the part, and it looks easy meat. They tell me that the French fliers never could withstand the temptation of seeing such a plane hovering round. The French flier would give chase, even far over the enemy lines, and at the very moment the Frenchman was about to attack under conditions that left but little doubt in his mind of the issue, unexpectedly, suddenly, he would find himself surrounded by three or four enemy planes of the latest model, with full armament.

"You see, the Germans would have been flying above the clouds, watching, the two planes below, and not showing themselves until the decoy plane had drawn the French flier ten or fifteen miles from his base. It pays to be mighty wary of anything that looks too easy in this game, and you can't be too much on the lookout for surprise parties when the clouds lie low."

"Tell us about the most exciting thing you have seen since you have been out here, Will," begged Dicky Mann. "I have been stuck on office work, and don't get a chance to have the fun the rest do. I would like to hear something about a real red-hot scrap that you have been in or seen."

"What work are you on?" queried Will.

"Maps."

"That isn't dull work, by a long shot. You can learn much in the map room that will be worth lots to you one day, too. A good knowledge of the country, the rivers, the canals, the railroads—-the ordinary roadways, for that matter—-has saved more than one chap from making a fool of himself."

"Dicky is as happy as a clam," said Harry. "He knows he is doing good work, and the amount of time he spends over his blessed maps shows well enough that he is out to get some of the map lore stuck in his head. Quit kicking, Dicky."

"All the same, you fellows have the fun," insisted Dicky. "I like the work well enough. I will admit that. And there are things worth picking up in that department, too. A man would be a fool not to see that. But tell us, Will, about the most exciting thing you have seen in the air."

There was a general seconding of Dicky's request, at which Will lit his pipe for the thirtieth time and said thoughtfully: "It is not an easy matter to choose, but the thing I had the hardest time to forget, and about the most spectacular thing a man could see, does not make much of a story. Like many things that take place in the air, it happened so quickly that we were unprepared for it.

"I was out with an observer, a very good pal of mine, on a big pusher-plane that had one of the finest engines in it I had ever seen. I don't know why we haven't had more of those out here. Something to do with the plane itself, I think. I understand the plane did not do so well as the engine, and they are getting out a new thruster to take that engine. When it comes along it will be a daisy. We had been doing what my observer called dog work. By that he meant just plain reconnaissance. We had taken in a given area, and followed all the roads to watch for traffic. We had noted nothing of particular interest, and at last we turned for home.

"We had not gone far when right ahead came a Boche flier pounding for home himself, apparently. It was a two-seater. He evidently liked our looks but little, and started to climb for safety. But we could climb, too. He had never met one of that pusher type, I guess. We kept on going up, getting higher and higher, and gaining on him all the time. It must have been a big strain for the men in that enemy machine.

"I could imagine them discussing us."

"What is it?" one may have asked.

"He will quit soon; we will be at twenty thousand feet before long," the other may have replied.

"It was at just about twenty thousand feet that we at last got within range. We had both been in chases before. We were cool enough about this one, I think. My observer was. He sat there calmly enough waiting till I could get near enough for him to let fly. I was too busy watching the fellow in front to think about much else. I have always thought that he must have miscalculated the distance that I had gained. Maybe something went a bit wrong with his engine that took his attention. He was about as far up as he could get his bus. Twenty thousand feet is nearly four miles, you know. We are likely to forget that. It is a long way up, even now, and it seemed further up then.

"I am afraid I am stringing the story out, rather, but it strung itself out that way. It was 'most all climb, climb, climb, with an eye on the two men in the plane ahead. Then I got him in range, and before I realized it." "Brrr-r-rr-rrr-rrrr!" started the quick-firer behind me. That was the most exciting moment I have gone through out here.

"They moment the machine-gun started something truly extraordinary happened. The Boche pilot, at the very first burst of fire from us, either jumped out of his seat or fell out.

"I could hardly believe my eyes. Yet there could be no mistake. He went over the side of his fuselage and dropped like a man who intended dropping just a few yards. I could see that he fell feet first, head up, and arms stretched up above his head, holding his body rigidly straight. Neither I nor my observer saw him the moment he left his seat, but both of us saw him leave the side of his machine and start down, down, down on that long four-mile drop.

"He disappeared, still rigidly straight, with something about his position that made us both remark afterwards that he looked as though he was doing it quite voluntarily and had planned it all out just that way. It was weird.

"Of course it all happened in a twinkling. The big plane in front of us went on uncannily, without a tremor, apparently. An instant afterwards my observer and I exclaimed loudly together. The observer in the enemy plane had not fired a shot, probably for the reason that his gun was fixed and we were never in range of it. Suddenly we saw him climb out of his seat on to the tail of the plane. My observer had a good target, but his gun was silent. Perhaps that Boche observer had an idea of climbing into the seat vacated so curiously by the pilot, dropping, dropping, dropping, down that trackless four mile path we had come up. If he had such a plan it failed almost before he started to put it into execution.

"He had no more than climbed out on the tail proper than he lost his hold and plunged headlong after his comrade. He went down pawing and clutching into the void below like a lost soul, in horrible contrast to the rigid figure of the pilot. Then the aviatik turned its nose down with a jerk and fell after its human freight, all the long twenty thousand feet to the earth below.

"We did not say a word to each other till we landed. It gave me a nasty shock. I had seen enemy planes go down with enemy fliers in them, but that rigid figure got me. The struggling chap I forgot long before I did the other. We more than once discussed what might have happened to him, and what his idea might have been—-but without being able to frame any explanation. It was just weird. We let it go at that."

As Will ended his story he pulled out his khaki handkerchief and wiped the perspiration from his forehead. The night was anything but warm, and the room in which they sat was quite cool; but the memory of that scene, four miles up, brought the moisture to Will's brow, after months had passed since the occurrence.

Two young officers in the mess had been interested listeners. One of them, a slight youth named Mason, who hailed from the Pacific Coast, now joined in the conversation.

"There has been an instance of an observer taking control of a plane and effecting a good landing after his pilot had been killed," said Mason. "He came down not a long way from an airdrome where I was stationed. A bit of anti-aircraft shrapnel caught the pilot in the back. It did not kill him instantly, but he was not long in succumbing to his wound. He had just energy enough left, after he realized that he was very badly hurt, to tell his observer that he was going off. Before he actually relinquished control of the machine, the observer, who was a daring chap, climbed right out of his seat, pulled himself along the fuselage, and half-sitting, half-lying, managed to stick there, within reach of the control levers and the engine cut-off.

"He was an old-time flyer himself, and understood aeroplane construction pretty well, and he made a very decent landing not very far from our front lines. Fortunately he was on the right side of them, though from what he told us afterward that was more luck than judgment. He thought he was much further back than he was.

"He had become very tired, owing to his strained position on the body of the plane, and was afraid he would fall off. So he came down. He had a bad shock when he found that his pilot was stone dead, and had been for some time. He must have died when the observer took over the control of the plane, but the observer, oddly enough, never thought of him as dead, and quite expected to be able to bring him around if he once got him safely landed."

"Well, that was enough to give anyone a shock," said Will. "But he would have had a worse shock if he had come down on the Boche's side. More than one chap has done that just through not knowing exactly where he was. I can't imagine anything more tough than to get yourself down when something has gone utterly wrong, thanking your lucky stars that you are down with a whole skin, and then discover you are booked for a Hun prison, after all. I could tell you a thriller along that line, but it'll keep. You've had enough now to make you believe that the Air Service demands of a man the very best there is in him, brawn and brain."

The hour was late before the boys knew the evening had passed, and they were most cordial in their invitation to Will Corwin to come and pay them another call. Will said he would do so when he could, but that next visit was to be long deferred.

Less than a fortnight later Will took part in a gallant fight against three machines that had attacked him far within the German territory.

He accounted for one, crippled another, and outsped the third—-but when he landed his machine in his home airdrome he settled back quietly in the driving seat as the machine came to rest. When his mechanics reached him he was unconscious!

Examination showed that Will had been hit by a machine-gun bullet, that had lodged in his shoulder. In spite of his wound, which was increasingly painful and made him fight hard to retain consciousness until he got home with his plane, he made a fine nose-dive that gave him a clear road to his own lines, and managed to dodge cleverly once on his way back when the German Archies began to place shells unpleasantly close.

Will was given much credit for his pluck and tenacity, was recommended for a special decoration, and was packed off to a hospital to recover from his wound, which fortunately gave the doctors little worry, though it put Will on his back for a long time.

CHAPTER IX

IN THE ENEMY'S COUNTRY

Dicky Mann became more interested in the study of maps and their making than he would have thought it possible. When he came sufficiently closely in touch with the intricate system by which the air-photograph and accurate map of every point behind the enemy line is carefully tabulated and filed away for reference, he developed a keenness for the work which made him a valuable member of the organization.

The Brighton boys found, as time went on, that they had, quite frequently, some spare hours in which they could do as they wished. Soon after their arrival in France they had envied Bob Haines his knowledge of the French language, which, while rudimentary, was sufficient to enable him to make himself understood at times when the boys were quite at sea as to what he was trying to say to the French people to whom he was talking.

No sooner had the boys noticed that Bob had a decided advantage over the rest of them on this score, than they set about to catch up with him. But Bob was equally set on keeping the lead he had gained. Joe Little and Dicky Mann were his only real rivals in this field. Dicky had one assistant that was of the greatest use to him in the frequent companionship of Dubois, the French officer attached to headquarters. While Dicky's French was often ungrammatical, his pronunciation was good, much better, in fact, than either Joe's or Bob's.

One day Dicky was sent as an observer with Richardson, the little major who usually accompanied that clever pilot being away on temporary leave. Dicky pleased headquarters so much with his initial report that more and more observation work was given him. Thus he gained valuable experience which bade fair to ensure that he would be kept at observing most of the time.

The boy was inclined at first to regret this, for the obvious reason that those who did the flying work were much more "in the picture," as Dicky put it, but the real fascination of the observation work soon weaned him from any genuine desire to give it up. To his great delight he was at last put on the observation staff permanently, or at least was given regular work with that department—-and who should be assigned to pilot him but Bob Haines! To be with Bob, of whom Dicky was especially fond, was a genuine pleasure to him, and the combination proved a very good one from every standpoint. Bob's passion for photographic work and Dicky's absorbing interest in mapping operations resulted in their approaching their joint work in a spirit of splendid enthusiasm for it, which could not but produce good results.

Aeroplane work in war-time, however, has its "ups and downs," as Jimmy Hill would say in his weekly letters home. He rarely missed a fortnight that this sage observation did not appear in some part of his four-page epistle. Jimmy stuck religiously to four pages, though he knew enough of censorship rules to avoid mention of his work, except in vague generalities. This necessity made writing four pages dull work at times, and resulted in Jimmy's adoption of various set phrases as filling matter. His mother, who knew Jimmy as only mothers know their sons, read into the often repeated sentences Jimmy's ardent desire to show himself a ready and willing correspondent, when he was nothing of the kind. She loved those letters none the less for their sameness, thereby showing her mother-wisdom.

Thus far in the career of the Brighton boys with the aero forces at the front their fortune had been on the side of the ups. The time came when the downs had an inning.

Bad luck overtook Bob Haines and Dicky Mann while on an observation flight far over the firing lines and well inside territory occupied by the enemy. They were on their outward journey, bound for a point which they hoped to photograph quickly and then run for home. The day was not an ideal one for flying, as shifting clouds gathered here and there, some high up, some low. When they were in the vicinity of their objective the clouds beneath them obscured their view to an annoying extent. They had seen no other plane, friend or enemy, since they had left their own lines. Suddenly, without the slightest warning, the engine stopped. Bob switched off the power, switched it on again, and repeated the maneuver again and again while volplaning to preserve their momentum.

Try as he would, he could not get a single explosion out of the motor. Of fuel he had plenty. His wires and terminals—-so much as he could see of them—-were apparently in good order, but the engine had just coolly stopped of its own accord, and could not be coaxed to start again.

Dicky looked round at Bob from the observer's seat in the fuselage and raised his eyebrows inquiringly. His glance fell on Bob's white, set face, and he saw that Bob was methodically going over one thing after another, and trying first this, then that, as if examining every part of the plane's mechanism that he could reach. They were still above the low-lying clouds that hid the earth.

"Engine?" queried Dicky.

Bob nodded. Still he ran his hands over the controls, as if loath to believe that he had exhausted every possibility of finding and rectifying the trouble. It was all in vain.

Still they swept lower and lower. Soon they would be below the clouds, and soon after that, landing so far inside the German lines that by no possibility could they hope to regain their own. It was a bitter time for Bob. Dicky, curiously enough, took the first realization of their predicament less hard. He was all eyes to see what fate had in store for them in the way of a landing place.

As they swept through the last bank of clouds and the country below spread before them, they saw that it was level pasture land for the most part, divided by green hedges, with here and there a cultivated field. A village lay some distance to the left, a mere cluster of mean houses. No chateau or large building was in sight, but small cottages were dotted about here and there in plenty.

"Not much room in one of those pastures," commented Dicky. "Mind you pick a decent one. Don't spoil the hedge on the other side of it, either."

Dicky's mood was infectious. Bob was sick at heart, but his friend's joking way of speaking had its effect.

"Would you rather be starved to death or neatly smashed? Do you prefer your misery long drawn out or all over in a jiffy?" Bob was joking now, though grimly enough.

"You tend to your part and let the Huns tend to theirs," answered

Jimmy.

They were almost down now. As they approached the field which Bob had chosen for landing, what was their horror to see, but one field away, two German soldiers in their field gray! They were armed with rifles, and appeared to be carrying full field kit.

No others were in sight. The two burly Teutons looked in amazement at the aeroplane, as if unable to grasp the fact that it was plainly marked with the red, white and blue circles stamping it as a machine belonging to the Allied armies.

While the boys knew well where they were, and how impossible it seemed that they could escape capture eventually, the sight of two German soldiers right at the spot upon which they had so unfortunately been compelled to land, was a real disappointment to them. Perhaps it was just such a disappointment, however, that was needed to key them up to prompt action.

Bob did not dare to try to clear the tall, thick hedge which separated the field he had chosen for a landing place from the one next to it. He must stick to his original intention. As he swooped down to the fairly level ground Dicky took one last glance at the pair of soldiers, who had started toward the point where they thought the plane would land. The question in Dicky's mind was as to whether or not the Boches would take a pot shot at the airmen before the machine came to rest. Evidently that had not occurred to them, however, and they merely started on a run, with the humane idea of taking the aviators prisoner.

The machine taxied the full length of the pasture and went full tilt into the hedge at the end of it. Luckily this hedge was just thick enough to stop the aeroplane effectively and yet prevent it from breaking through and capsizing. While the machine did not go on through the hedge, the two boys did. They crashed through and landed on the soft earth on the other side at almost the same moment. Each turned quickly to the other as they picked themselves up. Neither was seriously hurt, though Bob was badly shaken, and had scraped most of the skin off the front of both shins. Dicky's head had burrowed into the soft turf, and but for his aviator's cap he might have been badly bruised. That protection had saved him all injury save a skinned shoulder.

"Come on, let's give 'em a run for it!" yelled Dicky, who was first to recover his breath.

He started off, keeping close to the hedge, Bob close on his heels. As they approached the corner of the field they were faced with another hedge, evidently of much the same character as the one through which the boys had been hurled so unceremoniously a moment before. Inspired by a sudden thought, he put on a burst of speed, ran straight up to the leafy barrier, and dove right at it, head first as he used to "hit the center" for dear old Brighton. His maneuver did not carry him quite through, but he managed to wriggle on just in time to clear the way for Bob, who dived after him.

It was no time for words. Dicky started off to the right as fast as he could go, ever keeping close to the protecting hedge, running swiftly and silently over the grass, Bob not many feet behind. One hundred yards of rapid sprinting brought them to a lower, thinner hedge through which they climbed easily. Fifty yards away was a stream, which they jumped, finding themselves in a small wood. They made their way through this and debouched on a narrow country lane. The countryside seemed to contain no one except the two fleeing Americans and the two pursuing Germans. No sort of ground could have suited better the game of hide-and-seek they had started. Each time the Boches came to a hedge or a bit of brush they had to guess which way the Yanks had turned. Only once were they guided by footprints.

Fully accoutered and loath to throw off any of their equipment, the two Germans soon became thoroughly winded, and finally stopped short. They had no doubt lost some minutes at the start by warily examining the plane and all around it for signs of the former occupants, which had given the Brighton boys just the start they so badly needed.

But the lads were really but little better off when they came to the conclusion that they had, for the time, at least, shaken off their pursuers. They had passed fairly close to a cottage, which was apparently untenanted. Now they came upon another. No signs of life could they see around it. They pulled up for the first time and stood behind a rude shack nearby.

"Lot of good it will do us to run away from those two," growled Bob, panting. "If they don't find us some other Boches will. It is only prolonging the agony."

"I prefer the agony of being free to the agony of being a prisoner, just the same," replied Dicky. "Those two soldiers may have a job on that will not allow them to hang around here long. We have come quite a distance, and they would be very lucky to find us now. I'll bet they have gone on about their business. They will report the fact that a plane came down, and whoever comes to find it will think some other fellows have picked us up. This is too big a war for anyone to worry much about two men. Besides, the very hopelessness of our fix is in our favor."

"I don't mind looking for silver linings to the cloud," said Bob.

"But how you make that out I cannot see."

"Why, who would ever dream that we could get away? Who would even imagine it possible? Will the Germans spend much time searching to see if two Americans are hiding so far inside their lines? Of course not. They will think it absolutely impossible that we could get any distance without being picked up. Why should they waste their time over us?"

"Well, is that cheering?"

"You bet it is!"

"Do you mean that there is a chance that we will not be picked up?"

"Of course I do. Cheer up! We are not caught yet. Sicker chaps than we are have got well. True we can't get back to our front; and true again the chances are thousands to one against our escaping capture, but Holland is somewhere back of us and to the north—-and we have that one chance, in spite of all the odds."

"And what'll they do to us in Holland—-intern us for the duration of the war!" Bob was still pessimistic.

"Oh, you can't tell. If we can get away from the Boches we can surely get away from the easy-going Dutchmen—-and anyway, if we must be interned I'd rather it happened in Holland than in Hun-land. Let's play the game till time is called."

"You're right," said Bob. "I ought to be ashamed of myself for losing heart. Let's forget that we came down in that plane, and think of ourselves as pedestrians. I remember reading somewhere that if you want to play a part you've got to imagine yourself living it. Let's think we are Belgians."

"Good! And let's look like Belgians too—-I guess to do that we will have to turn burglar, eh? Well—-they say all's fair in love and war, you know. Come on! Let's break into this house and see what we can find?"

CHAPTER X

PLANNING THE ESCAPE

No breaking in was found necessary. The back door opened readily enough. The boys stepped into the rude kitchen and closed the door, listening for a moment in the silence. A meal of sorts was still spread on the plain deal table, but it had evidently been there for some days. The place seemed to have been deserted by its inhabitants without any preparation or warning. The stillness was uncanny, and Bob's voice sounded unusually loud as he remarked:

"Not even a cat left behind."

The poverty of the former occupants was apparent from a glance about the room, on one side of which was a half-cupboard, half-wardrobe, the open door of which showed sundry worn, dirty garments, little more than collections of rags.

"There is another room in front," remarked Bob. "From the look of things here, though, we can hardly expect to find any clothing that will serve our purposes."

Dicky stepped toward the door leading to the front of the building. "It is as silent as the grave, without a doubt," he said as he turned the handle and pushed gently. The door would not open.

"Stand back and let me shove," said Bob.

He put his shoulder against the door and threw his weight against it. The flimsy lock broke at the first strain, and Bob caught himself just in time to save himself from falling. No sooner had the boys gained an entrance to the room than they saw they were not the only occupants of it. On one side stood a low bed, upon which rested the wasted form of an old woman, her white hair pushed smoothly back from her forehead, but spread in tumbled disorder on the pillow.

The old woman was dead.

The locked front door showed she had shut herself in to die, and had died alone. How long she had lain there, as if asleep, for so she appeared, was a matter of conjecture. The thin, gnarled hands, brown with outdoor labor, were folded on her breast. Her face showed that calm with which death stamps the faces of long-suffering, simple-minded peasant folk. The patient resignation through the long years of toil, through years, perhaps, of pain and suffering, suffering more likely than not borne in silence, taken as a matter of course—-all seemed to have culminated in the quiet peace on the seamed dead face.

No wonder the boys involuntarily uncovered and stood for some time without speaking.

"Somebody's mother," said Dicky at last, with a catch in his throat as he uttered the words.

"Yes, perhaps," said Bob, as he gently covered the body with a blanket. "We must bury her decently. Who knows how long she might have lain here but for our chance coming?"

Under a dust sheet, strung on a bit of string along the side of the room, the boys found many women's garments, of the cheapest, simplest sort, and some men's clothing. Dicky stripped off his uniform and pulled on a random selection of what lay to his hand. With the addition of a dirty cap, found on the floor at the foot of the bed, and a pair of coarse boots, one without a heel, that were discovered in the cupboard in the kitchen, Dicky's disguise was complete. Given a plentiful application of dirt on face and hands, and a couple of days' growth of stubble on his chin, no one could have imagined him a smart young officer.

Bob was not so easy to outfit. His larger size made it impossible for him to find a coat that he could get into, so he had to content himself with an old shirt and a dilapidated pair of trousers which did not come near his feet. No other hat or cap could he find.

Toward dusk, at Dicky's suggestion, they went out and made a search for some rude instrument wherewith to dig a grave. They found a broken shovel and a dull adze-like implement. The grave prepared, and dusk having come, Bob was struck with the idea that they had best bury their uniforms.

"If the Germans should happen to clap eyes on us and decided to search us, it would be all up with two Brighton boys," said Bob. "So it's my think that we'd better hide the certain evidences as to our identity."

Dicky not only agreed to this, and started at once to put the idea into practice, but made a further suggestion. "We might give the poor old woman a better resting place further afield, if we knew where to find a graveyard," he said.

"We can search for one," replied Bob. "To carry her away from here would be the best plan, and bury her when we find a proper burial ground. We certainly should not have to take her far."

"If we were discovered doing so, I suppose the fact we were actually carrying our dead, or what the Germans would think was our dead, would help us to get a bit further, too," Dicky argued.

"Fine! And if I can't talk Belgian-French better than any German that ever lived I'll eat my helmet!"

So they took the cupboard door from its hinges, wrapped the body of the dead woman carefully in the tattered blankets from her bed, and laid it on the improvised stretcher.

"We should leave some sort of word as to what we are doing," said Bob.

"Suppose some of her folks come back and do not find any trace of her?

They might never know of her death."

"When we find a place to bury her we will find someone to whom we can tell her story, so much as we know of it," answered Dicky. "Perhaps we might even find a priest to help lay her away."

Thus, without definite plan except to beam their lifeless burden to some decent burial ground, the boys set out. They had not proceeded far along the lane that led away from the house when they heard voices. They plodded on, and passed a group of persons whom they took to be Germans from the deep gutturals in which they spoke. They were close to this group, too close for comfort, but passed unobserved in the gathering darkness.

For half an hour they bore the dead woman, passing houses at times, shrouded invariably in darkness. At last they came to a town. German soldiers were in evidence there, in numbers, but took no notice of the two bent forms bearing the stretcher. Bob, who was leading, bumped into a man in the dark.

"Pardon," said the man.

"Pardon, monsieur," replied Bob at once.

This was met with a soft-voiced assurance, in French that it was of no consequence, the remark concluding with the words, "mon fils."

"Are you the Father?" Bob blurted out in English.

"Yes," came in low tones in return. "I am Pere Marquee, my son. Say no more. You may be overheard. Follow me."

Around a corner, down a lane went Pere Marquee, the boys following with their strange load. Once well clear of the main street, the Father stopped.

"Speak slowly," he said. "I understand your language but imperfectly, my son."

Whereupon Bob promptly told him, in few words, of their quest. He told him, too, that they were American aviators in imminent danger of capture.

"Bring the poor woman this way," said the priest. He led them to a house which he entered without knocking, and asked them to enter. They took the dead woman into a room occupied by two old ladies, and set down their load as Pere Marquee hurriedly told the short story he had heard from Bob.

Dicky was nearest to the priest as he finished speaking and turned to the boys. The old man gave the young one a searching scrutiny, up to that time Dicky had not spoken.

"You, too, are American?" he asked, as if doubtful that so perfect a disguise could have been so hurriedly assumed.

Dicky's answer was short, and made in a tone and with an accent that made the good Father look still more sharply into the boy's eyes.

"No one would dream it," he murmured. "You are very like the poor dead woman's son—-so like that the resemblance is startling. It is no doubt the clothes that make me note it."

"Not altogether," interposed one of the old ladies. "His voice is strangely like that of Franois. I know, for Francois frequently worked here for us until they took him away. If the American would limp as Franois limped, most folk would take him for Franois, surely."

Franois, it was explained, had been hurt when a boy of twelve, and while not seriously crippled, always walked with a slight limp in the right leg.

Once having convinced their new-found friends that they were American soldiers whose object it was to restore Belgium to the Belgians, they all set about the discussion of what should be the next step.

Pere Marquee had known the dead woman. She had been ill for weeks, and he had been expecting to hear she had passed away. Too much was required of him in the village to allow of his leaving it to look after her.

The German colonel was not a hard man, "for a German," said the priest. The soldiers molested but little the townsfolk that were left. After some discussion the Father decided that the best plan would be to have a funeral in the morning, attended by the two American boys openly. Both spoke French sufficiently well to answer any questioning by the Germans. Dicky's disguise was perfect, they all declared. With the addition of the limp, which he decided to adopt, he might even fool some of the townsfolk. Before they lay down on the floor and snatched some sleep Bob's wardrobe had been replenished with old clothes gathered from a house nearby.

Little interest was taken in the funeral next morning so far as the Germans were concerned. For that matter but few townsfolk attended the actual interment. Those who did were very old folk or very young. Not one of them spoke to either Bob or Dicky. The whole affair seemed uncanny to the boys. Bob stooped as he walked at the suggestion of the priest, and Dicky's limp was very naturally assumed. No sharp scrutiny was given them, though each was bathed in perspiration when they regained the shelter of the house where they had spent the night.

"Not a moment must now be lost," said Pre Marquee. "You must get as far away from this village as possible without delay. Your presence here will lead to inquiry before many hours have passed, and subsequent registration. If that comes, you would be shot as spies without doubt, sooner or later. I advised that you take the chance of discovery at the funeral so that we could say that you came from a nearby town for that ceremony and had at once returned. Be sure that I shall select a town in the opposite direction to that in which you will be working your way. I am sure that the end justifies the means, and I wish you Godspeed."

Ten minutes later the two boys slipped out the rear door of the house. Dicky was soon limping through the trees of a thickly-foliaged orchard, Bob close behind. Stooping under the low branches, step by step they advanced. No one was in sight. A last glance behind and the boys ducked through the leafy hedge, wriggled over a low wall, and rolled into a deep ditch beside it. Stooping as low as they could, the boys followed this ditch for some hundreds of yards, until they were well clear of the town, and out of sight of anyone in it. Finally they reached a spot which seemed particularly well suited for a hiding place, and decided to remain there until dark before attempting to proceed further. All the rest of the day they lay in the moist, muddy ditch-bottom. Bob had torn a map from the back of an old railway guide he had seen in the house in which he had slept, and it was to prove of inestimable value to him. To strike north, edging west, and reach one of the larger Belgian towns was the first plan. What they should do once they had accomplished that, time must tell them. So far they had been blessed by the best of fortune, and the part of the country in which they had descended did not seem to hold very many German troops. Even Bob began to hope.

CHAPTER XI

THROUGH THE LINES

It was stiff, tiresome work lying quiet in the ditch that day, but with brambles pulled over them the boys were in comparatively little danger of discovery. At dusk they crawled cautiously out of their hiding-place and slowly headed northward. Every sound meant Germans to them, and their first mile was a succession of sallies forward, interspersed with sudden dives underneath the hedge by the roadside. The moon came up. The clank of harness and the gear of guns and wagons told of approaching artillery or transport, or both. From the shelter of the hedge the boys watched long lines of dusty shapes move slowly past. They seemed to be taking an interminable time about it. Now and then a rough guttural voice rasped out an order.

The boys waited for what seemed hours to them, and the very moment they would move, along would come another contingent of some sort. They had evidently struck a corps shifting southward. At last a good sized gap in the long, ghostly line gave them courage to cross. They got through safely enough, and kept on steadily for a time across country. They skirted two villages, and reached a haystack near a river-bank before daybreak. Out toward the east they saw the faint outlines of a fairly large town. Before them lay the river, spanned by a bridge guarded at each end by a German sentry. Hope fell several degrees.

The boys had climbed upon the stack and pulled the straw well over them. As they lay looking toward their goal, to the north, the home of the owner of the stack was at their backs. He made his appearance at an early hour, and came not far distant. After a whispered conference, Bob hailed him in a low tone. First the little man bolted back into his house without investigating the whereabouts of the mysterious voice. After a time he reappeared, and when Bob again sung out to him, he gingerly approached the stack, staring at it like mad, in spite of Bob's continuous warnings that he should not do so. Finally Bob induced him to mount the slight ladder by which the boys had climbed to their point of vantage.

He was a little man, with a thin red beard, great rings in his ears, and piercing, shifty eyes. A reddish, diminutive sort of man, altogether, with a thin little voice that went with his general appearance. He was literally scared stiff at the idea of the Boches finding the boys on his premises. That would mean his house burned, and death for himself, he said. Germans were all about, he said fearfully, and no one could escape them. He was so frankly nervous and so devoutly wishful that the boys had never come near him and his, that Bob, to ease the little man's mind, promised that the boys would swim the river when dark came and relieve the tension so far as the stack-owner was concerned. He was eager enough to see that the boys were well hidden, and before he climbed down the ladder he piled bundle after bundle upon them, as if preferring that they should be smothered rather than discovered by the dreaded Boches.

That was a tiring day, a hungry, thirsty day, but the boys lay as still as mice. From where they lay they could see a sufficient number of Germans passing and repassing along the road and across the bridge to hourly remind them of the necessity of keeping close cover.

At night, before nine o'clock, they climbed down from their hiding-place, went to the edge of the river, undressed, and waded out neck-deep. Dicky stepped on a stone that rolled over and in righting himself splashed about once or twice. In a moment a deep voice could be heard from the opposite bank, growling out, "Was ist das?" The boys kept perfectly still, and heard the German call out for someone to come. Quietly each of the boys ducked his head and gently waded back under water to the shelter of their own bank. There they sat, very cold and miserable, for some time. Then the moon came out and lit up the country-side bright as day.

"It's off for to-night," whispered Bob. "We must go back and have another try to-morrow night. That was bad luck. The Boche could hardly have been a sentry. I think he was just there by chance. What rotten luck!" So back they went, wet and cold, to their nest at the top of the stack, in anything but a hopeful frame of mind.

They fell into a sound sleep before long, and were awakened quite

early next morning by the weight of someone ascending the ladder.

"A Boche this time!" whispered Dicky as he regained consciousness.

"That light little man never could make such a commotion."

The perspiration broke out on Bob's forehead.

An age seemed to pass before the head of the intruder came into view. What was their surprise and relief to see the round smiling face of a Belgian woman of considerable size and weight! Redbeard had told her of his unwelcome guests and she had come to offer such succor and assistance as might lie in her power.

She was the widow of a Belgian officer, killed in the first fighting of the war. She asked if the boys were hungry, and when Bob admitted that they had been on very short rations indeed for some time she reached down and drew up a little basket containing a bottle of red wine and a plate of beans.

The Germans had taken most of the food in the district, and beans were her only diet save on those occasions when she managed to get some of the American relief food which a friend of hers had hidden away, drawing sparingly on the rapidly diminishing store.

It was a sad day for many folk in Belgium and Northern France, she said, when the American food stopped coming, but American soldiers should find that she remembered. As to getting across the river, she could guide the boys to a point where they might find it more easy to cross. She would return again at night and try to help them another stage their journey.

The day seemed brighter after the woman's visit. Night came at last, after an uneventful day of waiting, and with it the ample form of madame. She led the boys two miles eastward to where the ruins of a bridge still spanned part of the stream. Girders just below the water's surface made it possible to clamber across, she said, and there had not been a guard at that point for some months. The boys bade the good woman a very grateful good-by, and found the crossing much easier than they had expected to find it.

Soon they were plodding on by starlight, and by midnight had reached, unmolested, a road that seemed to lead due north. They went around all villages, and learned to consider dogs a nuisance in so doing. At first they were unduly nervous. Faint moonlight played strange games with their fancies. Once a tree-trunk held them at bay for some minutes before they discovered it was not a German with a rifle. It certainly looked like a German. A restless cow, changing her pasture, sent them flying to cover. A startled rabbit dashed across the road, and the boys flung themselves face downward in a gully in a twinkling. The night made odd, sounds, each one of sinister import to the fugitives. The wind sprang up and made noises that caused their hearts to jump into their throats half a dozen times.

The boys were sadly in need of food and drink. They decided to try the hospitality of some of the villages as they passed a hamlet. Approaching a house on the far side of a little cluster of dark dwellings, they lay by the door and under one of the windows for a few minutes, listening for the heavy breathing that might betoken German occupants. All seemed quiet and propitious, so Bob gave a gentle knock and explained in a low tone that two Americans, in hiding from the Germans, wished to enter. Sounds of commotion came from the cottage. A light flashed from a window, and a woman's shrill voice spoke the word "Americains" in anything but a low tone. A moment later, as they still waited for the door to open, a light appeared in the next cottage, and another feminine voice repeated the surprised ejaculation, "Les Americains!"

"Come on," said Dicky. "The sooner we get out of this the better.

That woman has raised the whole town."

The boys ran down the road quietly, but losing no time. Well it was that they did so, for they had not gone far before several shots were fired behind them, and one or two sinister bullets sang over their heads. They started running in good earnest then. Fortunately there was no pursuit. After a time they slowed down and again became a prey to all their former fears of night noises. A large bird flew close to Bob's head and gave him quite a scare. As they pressed on along the roadway, the clatter of hoof-beats coming toward them sent them to the roadside, where, a ditch offered welcome refuge.

Bob and Dicky jumped in, close together. At the bottom they hit something soft, which turned beneath them and gave a whistling grunt as their combined weight came down upon it. In an instant they realized that they had jumped full on top of a man. Who he was or what he was doing there was of no moment to the boys. A sound from him might mean their capture. Bob grabbed the man, grappled with him in the pitch dark, and choked him into unconsciousness, Dicky lending a hand. A troop of German cavalry clattered up. Just as the troop drew abreast, the order was given for them to slow from a trot into a walk. The boys held their breath. Gradually the horsemen drew past, then away. Bob waited until they were well in the distance, and then examined the poor fellow underneath. If the boys had been scared to have jumped on the man, the man had been more than scared to have had them do so.

There was all-round relief when the boys found the victim to be an elderly Belgian farmer; and the relief of the farmer himself as he gathered his scattered wits, to find that the boys had no designs further upon his welfare, was truly comic. The Germans, he said, had imposed severe penalties on inhabitants who roamed about the country-side between eight o'clock in the evening and daylight. His quest remained unexplained, except in so far as a sack of something the boys did not examine might have explained it. Bob advised the old man to remain where he was till morning light, and the boys pressed on.

Before dawn they took refuge in a shed behind a house whose stately lines were marred by the marks of bombardment.

The owner of the half-ruined house and the shed where they had taken refuge proved to be a fine old Belgian, courageous and full of resource. As soon as he found that the boys were escaping American airmen he brought food and drink to them in plenty. They were a long way from the Holland line, he said, but they might, with care, get across. Others had done so. He would look into the probabilities and possibilities, and let them know.

The shed was a bare, small building of rude boards, with nothing in it. A few boards were placed across the eaves, forming a sort of loft extending for some seven feet from the end of the building. It was on these boards that the boys spent their days while waiting for an opportune moment to go further. Their host would not hear of their suggestions that they should leave the shed until he had arranged plans for their reception at a further station on their journey.

"I wonder why he does not ask us to come into his house?" queried Dicky after the boys had been two days in the shed. "It seems to be big enough—-even what's left of it—-to have plenty of hiding places in it, judging from what I can see of it out of this hole in the roof."

"He probably has his reasons," was Bob's reply.

That he had was proven the next day, when a squad of German soldiers came and spent an hour searching the house. One of them glanced in the doorway of the shed, but did not come inside. Seeing the bare surroundings, it evidently did not occur to him to glance upward. That night, when the Belgian brought their food, he told them that his house was searched periodically, though as yet no one had been discovered in hiding there.

Impatiently, they spent a week on the hard boards of the loft in the shed. At last their host was ready for them to move on. He gave them a map of the country, on which he marked the route and their stopping places. After six hours' steady march through a driving downpour they found another shed, in just the place that had been described to them before starting. It, too, had a hospitable loft, and food was there in plenty.

Two more stopping places, always in sheds or outbuildings, and they were very near that part of the Dutch frontier which their friends, most of them unknown, were planning that they should cross. Money, they were told, was to be a factor in their obtaining entrance to Holland. They knew little of the detail of what happened. They were guided one night by a dwarfed cripple to a little wood, and there spent four hours in weary waiting in absolute silence. Then the cripple returned and motioned them to follow him. This they did, and when they reached the edge of the wood, commenced crawling on all fours, as their guide was doing.

They crawled for some hundreds of yards, winding about the scrub brush and tall grass, and then suddenly came upon a wire fence. A dark shape loomed up on the far side of this barrier. The cripple, aided by the man on the other side, held apart two strands of the wire, and cautioned the boys to step quickly through the opening.

The cripple disappeared in the black night, the dark form beside them motioned in a ghost-like way to the blackness ahead of them, and without a sound they pressed on, as though in a dream, hardly daring to hope all would come out well.

By daylight they were able to distinguish something of the general outlines of the country, which was flat, damp and fog covered. A tall line of poplars led them toward a road. As they reached it, in the gray of the morning, Bob turned to Dicky and said the first words either of them had spoken for more than an hour.

"Do you think we are really in Holland, and free?" he queried.

"The whole thing was done in such a mysterious fashion, and silence so rigidly enjoined by everybody, that I would not be surprised if we have been smuggled out of Belgium, Bob," was Dicky's reply.

Nevertheless, they were most cautious as day came. They hid for a time, then decided to go to some homely cottage and see what manner of folk they would find. Stealthily approaching a simple home, they waited until they caught sight of the housewife who was outside it, feeding her chickens.

"She looks Dutch," said Dicky. "Let's try her."

They came upon her suddenly, but she showed no great surprise. Perhaps she had seen escaping soldiers of the Allied Armies in that part of the world before. She could not understand either English or French, but offered the boys a drink of milk and some bread, taking the money they proffered for it and looking at the coins curiously before she placed them in her pocket.

"She is Dutch as Dutch," was Bob's conclusion.

Sure enough, they were in Holland at last.

Careful maneuvering enabled them to get a passage to England, though they had to use camouflage in their answers to certain pointed questions in order not to disclose the fact that they were American belligerents.

It was not until their arrival in London—which they reached without further incident—that something of their real adventures became known.

Bob voted that they proceed at once to Farnborough, which he had heard was the headquarters of the British Flying Corps. An English intelligence officer who had helped them to get through from Holland had suggested Farnborough, too. Accordingly they wasted no time in London, except to inquire for the whereabouts of the Farnborough train. They were soon at Waterloo Station, and by afternoon had come to the Royal Aircraft Factory Grounds, which were then at Farnborough. There the commander was very cordial to them, and found a place for them to get a bath in a jiffy. More than once the boys had effected changes of raiment during their series of adventures, but while they did not look quite as bad as they did when they assumed their first disguise in France, they were still dressed in odd fashion. Two smart British uniforms were given them, and they were told that they would be very welcome and honored guests at the general's mess for dinner.

At dinner they told their story in relays, to an intensely interested audience. It was voted a truly great adventure, and the two young Americans were overwhelmed with genuine admiration from their British comrades.

"I suppose your squad have no idea you escaped, have they?" asked the general, who was a very youthful man for his rank.

"I dare say they imagine we are done for," answered Bob. "I think we should send word to them as soon as we can."

"We have a squadron of pushers going over in the morning, sir," remarked the commander to the general, "and if these boys would like to get over to their own crowd in a hurry they could take a couple of that new squadron over for us. We are really very short-handed. It would help us and it might suit the boys. It would be quite dramatic for them to show up over there in person after being counted as lost. How would it suit you, gentlemen?"

Both of the boys though it a splendid idea, and as the general good-naturedly acquiesced, they went to bed early to get up at dawn and have a trial flight on the two machines which they were to pilot across the channel.

The new machines were in fine trim, and the whole group were in France, at the appointed time and place in due course. The airdrome where the squadron landed was but four hours' drive by motorcar from the point from which Bob and Dicky had started the flight that had ended so strangely for them. The flight commander of the Britishers gladly sent the American lads to their own airdrome in a car, and they arrived at dinner-time. When they walked into the headquarters' hut they had a welcome indeed, and half an hour later when they were allowed to join their comrades in the mess building, there was a scene that none of the Brighton boys could ever forget. Feeling ran too deep to make any of the fellows try to hide wet eyes, and lumps in the throat made handclasps all the more firm.

Bob and Dicky were anxious to know how the rest had fared during their absence, but not a word would anyone of the others say until the two returned heroes of the mess had gone over their story in detail.

As the boys finished the recital of their adventures Joe Little expressed the universal feeling in the hearts of every one of the Brighton boys when he turned to Bob and Dicky, and putting a hand on a shoulder of each, said soberly: "Fellows, if two of us can get out of a hole like that and get back safe and sound, we can rest mighty secure in the sort of Providence that is looking after us. It is little we need to worry about what may happen to us, after all."

"You never know how lucky you can be in this world," said Bob.

"And you never want to be afraid to give your luck a fighting chance," added Dicky.

CHAPTER XII

PLUCK AND LUCK

No little change came over the Brighton boys as they developed into seasoned fighting airmen. They looked older, harder, but they were just as much boys as ever.

The first serious casualty suffered by their little band of six came to Archie Fox. Archie was doing what he called "daily grind" when Fate overtook him. That "daily grind" was the sort of work that bid fair to end in disaster one day or another.

Well Archie remembered that day. It had started much the same as other days experienced by Archie's unit. The getting ready of the machine, the brief examination of the controls, first Archie and then his observer, a young officer named Carleton, taking their seats, the word given, and then all other sound shut out by the dull roar of the engine—-it was always like that. Lines of trees, patchwork patterns made by the fields, and oddly grouped farm buildings swept along beneath the soaring plane, growing smaller with uncanny rapidity. The day's work started. That was all it amounted to. In the airdrome they had left behind, the eyes that had followed their first moments of flight were turned to other sights nearer at hand. The men who had seen the plane well away started for other jobs, forgetting the departed machine.

Both Archie and Carleton, neither novices at the game, settled themselves snugly in their seats as the needle crept round the altimeter. Cold awaited them in the higher levels. That they knew. A persistent, penetrating cold, driven by a keen wind right through some great-coats. Leather is the best protection from that sort of wind. The face feels it the most, however. The cheeks become cold as ice. Far below, the snakelike windings of trenches—-trenches of friend and foe—-can be followed from high altitudes. Some parts of the line seem mile-deep systems of trenches, section on section, transverse here, approach line there, support line behind, ever joining one with another in wondrous fashion. Shell-torn areas between the trench lines, the yellow earth showing its wounds plainly from well above, caught the eyes of the fliers.

The bark of a bursting anti-aircraft shell heralded their arrival in the danger zone. From the earth the tiny white shell clouds have a fascination for the onlooker. More so perhaps, than for the man in an aeroplane, not many yards distant from the bursting shrapnel. The ball of fluff that follows the sharp "bang" is small at first, but unrolls itself lazily until it assumes quite a size. That morning the anti-aircraft gunners seemed unusually accurate. The third shell burst not far below the plane, and two bits of the projectile punctured the canvas with an odd "zipp." Some shells came so close that the explosions gave the machine a distinct airshock, though no other shell struck the plane.

Archie swung his plane now this way now that to render the aim of the "Archies" below ineffective, smiling to himself, to think that the nickname given to the anti-aircraft guns was his own given name.

"We are providing amusement for a pretty big audience, below there," thought Archie. "I suppose that the closer they come to us with those shells the better sport it is for those who are watching us."

He laughed quietly at the thought. He was as cool as possible that day. In fact, he was unusually cool, for oftentimes the salvo of bursting "Archies" all about him would make his nerves tighten a bit. That morning he was at his best. He felt a calm confidence in his machine that made flying her a real pleasure. It even added spice to the flight to know they had to pass so dangerous a locality before reaching the area which was their objective. Over that area his observer was to hover sufficiently long to be able, on returning, to concoct a reliable and intelligible summary of what had come within his line of vision.

Carleton was soon busy with his glasses. A group of cars on a siding near a station were carefully counted. A line of horse transport on a country road was given considerable attention. Working parties along a small waterway were spotted and located on the map. A score of motor lorries, advertised by a floating dust cloud, scurried along below, to duly come under Carleton's eye and be at once tabulated by him for future reference. At one railway station a sufficient amount of bustle caused Carleton to watch that locality carefully.

"That is odd," he mused. "New activity there this morning. Maybe the Boches have planned an ammunition dump at that point. That is one for the bombers."

Thus time passed. Archie was busy dodging his dangerous namesakes, while Carleton focused his entire attention on gathering material for his report.

Carleton did not watch the movements below, however, with more care than Archie watched the sky on all sides for signs of enemy air-craft. The American machine had been so long inside the enemy lines that a German fighting plane might be expected at any moment. At last a Boche plane did make its appearance, a mere brown speck, at first, far ahead. Archie's signal to Carleton that trouble was ahead was conveyed by giving the machine a slight rock as he started to climb. Not much time was allowed for maneuvering. Carleton lost no time in placing a disk on his Lewis gun, and as the German approached, both observers opened up with a salvo. It was all over in a second. Firing point blank, in that fraction of time spent in passing, both had missed.

The excitement of that brief encounter, a mere matter of seconds as the two swift planes swept out of each other's range, was hardly past when the rattle of a machine-gun nearby and the zipp! zipp! as the bullets tore their way through the canvas, told of another Boche machine at hand. Neither Archie nor Carleton could see it. Carleton unbuckled the strap that held him in his seat, rose, and looked over the top plane.

There, just above and well out of range, was an enemy fighting plane. The machine had apparently dropped from the clouds above, and with great good fortune gained an ideal position. Before Archie could swing his "bus" around so that Carleton could get his Lewis gun to work on the Boche another salvo came from the enemy machine-gun.

That belt of cartridges found its mark. Both Carleton and Archie were hit, the former badly. The young officer dropped back into his seat. Archie saw that the lad had sufficient presence of mind to hastily buckle his belt round his waist again, then, his right shoulder numb, he dived steeply, bringing his plane up and straightening it out after a sheer drop of a thousand feet.

The German machine tail-dropped after the American one, but by a stroke of good luck the enemy pilot seemed to have some difficulty in righting. When Archie headed for home the Boche flier was far below.

Carleton had become unconscious. Archie's head began to swim. His right arm became stiff, and the blood from a wound in the shoulder trickled down his sleeve. He dared not try to stop the bleeding, and decided to trust to luck and make for home as fast as he could. Periodically he became dizzy and faint, and once, when he thought he was going to lose consciousness, he was roused by an anti-aircraft shell that burst but a few feet from one of his wing tips. He managed to dodge about and tried a half circle to get out of range of the guns below.

Archie felt cold and hot by turns. Then his arm became painful. The pain was all that made him keep consciousness, he thought afterward. At last his own lines were passed. He felt a strange weakness, and began to lose interest. Carleton's inert body swayed to one side, and called Archie's attention to the fact that he was custodian of another life, as well as his own, if life was still in Carleton's body. Archie felt, somehow, that Carleton was not dead. That thought keyed him up to still greater effort. He throttled his engine and started downward, the warmer airs welcome as he came lower. At last he was in home air. A final decision to buck up and hang on was necessary to urge his weak muscles to act. He swayed in his seat. His eyes closed and his grasp on the levers slackened. Again he saw that senseless form strapped in the observer's seat. Poor Carleton. He had been hard hit. Nothing for it but to land him as gently and as safely as possible. Will power overcame the growing weakness and inertia for one more struggle against the darkness that threatened his consciousness, and Archie, striving with every element of his being against falling forward insensible, threw back his elevator and made a good landing.

As the machine came to rest the mechanics ran up to it and found both observer and pilot apparently lifeless in their seats. Willing hands soon had the two young men out of the machine and in the orderly tent under the eye of the doctor. Carleton was the first to regain consciousness. He was sorely wounded, a machine-gun bullet having struck him in the neck and another in the leg. Archie's wound was not so bad, but the hard fight to keep going and bring Carleton and himself back home safely had told on his nervous system. At last he opened his eyes, and smiled to hear his C.O., who was standing beside him, say: "Carleton says you both got it well on the Boche side of the line, and that you must have done wonders to get away and get home. We won't forget your pluck, young fellow. Now let them take you away and patch you up as soon as they can."

It was not often that the chief distributed praise, which made it the more sweet. Archie was sent back to hospital, to spend many weary weeks there, but to come out well and fit again at last. Carleton was much longer in the doctor's hands, and months passed before he again saw the front.

CHAPTER XIII

THE RAID ON ESSEN

A new triplane of great climbing power and high speed came to the airdrome. Joe Little fell in love with it. Twice he took it on bombing expeditions and twice returned with reports of real damage to enemy supply stations and communications.

One night round the dinner table the boys of Joe's squadron planned a raid of some magnitude, and later asked permission to carry it into effect. It was a scheme to drop a load of bombs on the great Krupp works at Essen. This had been done by one or two individual fliers from Allied units, but the boys planned that with six of the new type triplanes, if they could be procured, a really effective raid on the great German productive center could be carried out.

The commanding officer did not disapprove the idea, but passed it above him for approval from headquarters. The boys had worked out the details carefully, and were keen on their project. At last permission came. Booth, one of the most experienced aviators on the western front, was to pilot one of the two triplanes of the new type that had been allotted to the airdrome, and Joe Little the other. The four other big bombing machines that were to go on this mission were to be sent from another air station nearby. Joe was pleased to be able to take Harry Corwin as his companion, and none of the twelve men who had been selected for the expedition worked harder over the plans and the maps than these two Brighton boys.

At last the night selected for the raid came. It was a study to see Joe Little inspect a machine before a flight, but on this occasion he went over the big plane with extra care. He stood by the right side of the tail for a minute chatting to Harry and then the two boys went over every detail of the machine. While one fingered the tail skid bolt the other examined the safety cable on the tail skid. Stabilizer, elevator, and rudder were gone over carefully. Control wires were gone over for their full lengths and their pulleys tried. Brace wires were felt for slackness, from the tail to the inside of the fuselage. The control wires to the ailerons, the pulleys and the hinges, nothing escaped the eyes of Joe Little.

Each blade of the propeller he searched for a minute crack. Every nut and bolt on the propeller he tried.

When in the machine and safely buckled to their seats, Joe ran his engine a bit, to satisfy himself that she was producing just the right music. The other five triplanes had been waiting. When Joe had satisfied himself that his machine was in perfect condition the word was given for the start. A series of staccato pops announced that the whole fleet was getting under way and they were soon circling the hangars and climbing off in the direction of the trenches. The long journey had begun.

The night was moonlit and the stars were bright. Not a cloud was to be seen. A fog obscured some of the low ground over which the squadron had to pass, but they steered by compass, keeping perfect formation. Finally the silver Rhine wound below them. Turning, they followed the river until Coblenz was reached, then turned north again. Germany's great manufacturing centers were passing below the squadron now, one after another. The countless fires of monster furnaces and factories, thousand upon thousand, glared into the night. The tall chimneys and furnace stacks belched forth red, yellow, and white flame as the munition works were pressed to their utmost to produce the sinews of war for the guns along the line over which the squadron had come.

By a certain point of identification all of the fliers knew Dusseldorf when that large factory center was reached. So far they had not seen an enemy plane. Essen was not far ahead now. Searchlights had been semaphoring over more than one town they had passed, but not until they had come over Dusseldorf did any of the Hun eyes from below see them. At Dusseldorf they were spotted and a veritable hail of anti-aircraft shell was hurled skyward. The signal to climb higher was given and they were soon out of reach of the "Archies."

As they approached Essen the fires from thousands of furnaces lit up the whole country round. Below them was the very heart of shell-production and gun-making. The sight was an awe-inspiring and magnificent one. The lights were so bright that the pilots and observers could hardly distinguish the flashes of the guns which were firing hundreds of shells at the menacing squadron.

Hovering but a few seconds above the scene of so much activity, guided by the flaring furnaces and the blazing chimney stacks far beneath, the signal was given to release the bombs, and down through the night air, into the fire and smoke, dropped bomb after bomb.

As they fell and exploded their flashes could be seen distinctly in spite of the blaze all about them. Great tongues of flame licked up heavenward as if trying to reach the aircraft that had hurled the destruction down upon the seething hives. A dull boom told of an explosion, and the air rocked with the disturbance.

Hundreds of pounds of high explosive fell on Essen that night. Great fires started here and there, visible to the Americans long after they had started for home, which they did as soon as their loads of bombs were loosed on the factories and munition plants beneath. Enemy planes had begun to climb up to engage the daring raiders, but the triplanes were well away before the German fliers reached anything like their altitude. Not one of the six bombers had been hit. Back they flew, satisfied that damage had been wrought to the enemy plants, back by the Rhine and the Moselle, back safely to their aviation base.

At last, ahead, the pilots could see the flares lit to guide their return. Each flier switched on his little light to see his instruments, and gracefully dropped nearer the ground. A night landing is always interesting. The familiar points near the airdrome have a strangely different appearance at night. Everything is vague in outline—-indistinct. Down the six machines dropped to the rows of lights, flickering in the night breeze. A last moment, then the instant for raising the elevator, then the gentle, resilient bump as the wheels touch the level floor of the airdrome, and the fleet is home.

It was a fine raid, well planned and splendidly executed. It did not cost our side a man nor a machine, and it spread death and destruction among the centers that turned out the means of destruction that had made the world-war a thing of horror. To bomb Krupp's works! The very thought had a ring of retribution to it! The very name Krupp had so sinister a sound. Well might the Brighton boys be proud of Joe for the part he had played in the inception of the idea and the work of carrying it through. They were proud. So was Joe's mother when she heard of it. Harry Corwin wrote home about it. He wrote three times, as a matter of fact, before he could concoct an account of the night flight that would pass the censor. Finally he accomplished that feat, however, and thus Joe Little's mother heard of what her boy had done. The brave woman cried a little, as mothers do sometimes, but her eyes lit up at the thought of the lad distinguishing himself among so many brave young men. Such a son was worth the sacrifice, she thought, with a sigh. "He is his father's son," she said to herself. And to her came his words, spoken many months before, "And my mother's," and her heart swelled with pride.

CHAPTER XIV

A FURIOUS BATTLE

For a time it seemed that the Brighton boys were doomed to be separated, but word came to the squadron commander in some way of the manner in which they had entered the service, and he so arranged matters that they were retained in his unit. Moreover, he saw to it that their work should so far as possible keep them in touch with each other.

News came one day that the squadron to which they belonged was before long to be transferred to the rear for a well-deserved rest, and a new lot was to take their place. The boys were speculating upon this item of news one evening after dinner, when Joe Little said: "What a fine thing it would be if one day we all went out on the same job! Did you fellows ever come to think of the fact that the whole lot of us have never actually been out together once since we came to France? I would like to see the whole lot of us have a shot at the Boches at the same time, before we quit."

"I had a letter from Archie to-day," said Jimmy Hill. "He says it will be some time before he rejoins us."

"Well, five of us are here yet, thanks more to luck than good sense," laughed Joe. "I think the Boche would know the five of us were left if we went out together and had a smack at him."

"Stranger things might happen," said Richardson, looking up from an illustrated paper. "The chief was talking only yesterday about sending out a combined bombing and observing expedition to save hunters. Three pilots gone sick in three days has made him short, he said. I think the lot of us want a rest, if you ask me. With three more fellows down there will not be such a lot of hunter pilots to choose from. So you wonderful birds may have that chance to show off that you're worrying about."

This sally raised a general laugh, and Bob Haines said quietly: "If a bunch goes out to-morrow and we are all in it, I for one certainly hope that you are in it, too, Richardson. I do not see any harm in thinking we are better than the German fliers. I believe we are, and I would like nothing better than to have one good combined go at Brother Boche before we leave this part of the line."

Bob said this in such a serious tone that Parker, who had come in late and was devouring a huge plate of corned beef.—-"bully," as he called it—-and a big pile of bread and butter, looked up and nodded his approval. "Me, too," Parker said, between bites.

"What we want and what we will get may be two very different things," said Harry Corwin. "We have never built any castles in the air yet that materialized. I guess our combined raid, much as we might enjoy it, will be a long time coming."

Harry was wrong. Two days later, the flight commander received orders to carry out certain observation work and certain bombing work in the same sector of the enemy's territory. The two new triplanes were to be used as a bombing machine and an observation machine respectively. The flight commander assigned the piloting of the first machine to Richardson and the second to Bob Haines. To Bob's delight Dicky Mann was chosen as his observer. Four of the wasp-like hunter machines, the swiftest planes in the airdrome, were to accompany the two triplanes. The pilots selected for these four one-man fliers were Parker, Jimmy Hill, Joe Little and Harry Corwin.

The six machines were in the air before the boys realized that they had their wish of two nights before. The roar of the six engines filled the airdrome. Circling up, before the planes had risen more than a few hundred feet, they began to take up their respective positions according to instructions. The two heavier machines hung comparatively low, while the four hunters, light and agile, climbed higher and higher, above and on each side of the larger machines below them. The great wing spread of the triplanes, and the huge, ugly fuselage of the bombing machine, were in sharp contrast to the dainty, wasp-bodied hunters.

Richardson's little major sat behind the machine-gun that was mounted on the front of the fuselage of the big bombing machine. There were sufficient high explosive bombs at his feet and suspended around the cock-pit of the fuselage to do great damage if properly directed. Dicky Mann was perched out on the very nose of the observation plane. On one side of him was his Lewis gun, on the other his camera. The great power of the triplanes had made it possible for the fuselage on each one to be lined with light splinter-proof armoring, which gave the occupants an added sense of security.

The four hunters sailed high out of sight of the two big triplanes. It was a day of spotted clouds, a day of a sort of hide-and-seek in the air. Up twenty thousand feet, nearly four miles above ground, the quartette made for the appointed place, then took up their positions and circled round waiting for developments.

Bob and Dicky, in the observation plane, were after certain definite photographs, and the lower cloud strata made it necessary for them to drop lower than usual to obtain that of which they were in search. The Boche "Archies" burst shells all about them, but Bob kept the swift machine maneuvering in such manner that to hit it required great good fortune on the part of the German gunners. The pop! pop! pop! of the anti-aircraft shrapnel and the whizz! of the pieces of shell went almost unnoticed by the two boys, so intent were they on their quest. Once bits of shell tore through one of the planes, and once a few stray bits rattled against the light armor of the fuselage.

Richardson and the major, in the other triplane, had climbed to a greater height. Richardson's instructions were to get into a certain position as soon as possible and drop several hundred pounds of high explosive on a big munition dump. Experience had taught him that to be at a good height above an exploding dump was advisable. Once before he had nearly been wrecked by the explosion of a German munition depot, which had caused a commotion in the air for thousands of feet above it.

Just as Bob and Dicky were circling around the spot they were bent on photographing, and Richardson and the major were loosing off their messengers of destruction toward the munition dump they had set out to destroy, the four men in the hunters, at twenty thousand feet, were beginning to feel the cold. Parker, whose job it was to give the signals for action to his little fleet, dipped his plane slightly and peered downward to see what was taking place below. His face felt as if it was pressed to a block of ice. Surely some enemy scouts would be on hand soon.

As Parker circled round, his eyes searching the sky below him, seven

Boche fighting machines came hurtling down from the north.

They had been hidden by fleecy, spotty clouds for a few moments, and were already too near to the two triplanes below. Parker waved his wing tips, which was his signal to his three companions in the hunting machines that the fight was on, and headed toward the oncoming fleet of seven. Joe Little was the first of the other three to see their adversaries, and was not far behind Parker. Next came Jimmy Hill, with Harry Corwin bringing up the rear.

The splendid planes rushed to the attack as though they knew the necessity for speed. Their engines purred smoothly, singing a vicious song, as they worked up their speed to more than a hundred miles an hour. The four American hunters were high above the seven German machines. Then the time came to drop downward. Parker first, and the other three in turn, dipped the noses of their planes. The added assistance of gravity lent swiftness to their flight until they were swooping down on the enemy at little less than one hundred and fifty miles an hour. The Boches at first seemed so intent upon their quarry, the two triplanes, that they were like to be taken completely by surprise by the four wasps from the upper air. Then they saw the descending quartette. Parker, ahead, with one hand on his controls and the other on his Lewis gun, made direct for the first Boche of the seven. The moment he was within range he opened fire.

Parker was going at such speed that the fifty rounds he loosed off apparently missed his opponent, in spite of the fact that but forty yards separated them when the last bullet left Parker's gun. The German went down in a clever spiral for a couple of thousand feet. When he flattened out, however, Parker, who had dived with and after him, was close behind. More, he was in an ideal position, from which he fired another fifty rounds. These steel messengers reached their billet, and the German flier went straight down to earth.

But while Parker had been dropping with eyes on the first Boche, the second had dropped after Parker. Parker reached for a new drum for his Lewis gun, and as he did so the second Boche, who had got on Parker's tail, let go at close range. The hunter was riddled. Parker felt that he was hit, but not badly. That was his impression, at least, at the moment. He spun his hunter round and dropped sheer for a thousand feet, coming up in a fairly thick bank of white cloud. He there flattened out again and began climbing, not being sure of his altitude. No sooner had his engine begun to drone out the rhythm of its full power, and the good hunter-plane begun to rise majestically, than what should he see but the second enemy fighter right in front of him! A new drum was in place on his Lewis gun, and he let go. The Boche pilot threw up both hands and fell back, and down into the cloud went the enemy plane, clearly out of control and quickly out of sight.

Parker examined himself as well as he could, but was unable to locate his wound. It was in his back somewhere, for he felt a stiffness and numbness all down his spine, but he still could move his arms, and felt no faintness. He decided that it must be merely a scratch, and climbed up as fast as he could to get into the fray again.

The other three American hunters had engaged in close, desperate encounters to a man. Joe Little was lucky enough to bring down his adversary and circled round toward the two triplanes, which had both finished their work and were climbing fast to get out of the range of the "Archies." Jimmy Hill had missed his man, who went down in a spiral, Jimmy spinning down after him. Owing to the greater pace at which Jimmy was traveling he had to make a wider spiral. The Boche flattened out and Jimmy dived for him again, but before he could come within range the German dived straight down to the ground and safety, where he appeared to land in such manner as to show that he had suffered but little, if any, damage. Jimmy was treated to an exceptionally severe salvo of "Archies" before he could get well up again, and was slightly wounded in the cheek by a shrapnel splinter. Harry Corwin's adversary fired at Harry, and Harry fired at him, but neither made a hit, so far as could be seen. The Boche was soon lost in a cloud for which he was heading, and Harry circled back to find his fellows.

Meantime two of the German fighting machines had kept on for the big triplanes. They were heading for fast, powerful machines, well armed, but they dashed at them as though they had no fear of result. The first German machine to score a hit was a fast Albatros. It dived straight at Richardson's machine. Richardson side-slipped and dropped like a stone till close to the ground. Not a single German who watched his drop, whether watching from the air or from the ground, dreamed that the big machine was still under control. Just before it seemed about to crash into the earth, however, Richardson righted it, and heading for home, skimmed the ground at a height of not more than fifty feet above the ground. The doughty little major poured round after round of bullets from his machine-gun at the heads of the Huns in the trenches and dugouts as the fleeing plane passed close over the astonished Germans, and the whole thing was over before anyone except the two occupants of the plane realized what was taking place.

Not a single shot from the thousands fired hit the brave young pilot, though the major was not quite so fortunate, having been wounded in the wrist by a ball from the machine-gun of the flier who attacked them from the Albatros. How they escaped death at his hands they hardly knew, for he had poured a veritable storm of lead into them at close range, and made dozens of holes in one or other of the three planes. Richardson's arrival with the major at the home airdrome was the first news to come back of the fight in the air. The major reported that they had satisfactorily performed their part of the work and escaped with but little damage. The Boche ammunition dump they were to assail had been blown into a thousand fragments, the detonation of the explosion having been heard for miles.

Meanwhile, Bob Haines and Dicky Mann in the other triplanes were having an exciting fight with another Albatros. Bob had chosen to meet the Boche attack head on. Dicky was a good shot, and tried his best to wing their fleet antagonist, but failed to hit him. Perhaps the readiness of the two Americans to meet the attack, however, had somewhat disconcerted the German's aim, for he too, missed the triplane.

The spotty clouds made the fighting in-and-out work that morning. The four hunters were still in commission, as was the observation triplane. Three Boche fliers of the seven had been accounted for, and a fourth driven down. Things looked very good for the Brighton boys, but they were over enemy territory and by no means "out of the woods" yet. A speedy Boche trio which had apparently not before seen the Americans suddenly dived from a good height and the fight began all over again.

In the melee of looping, side-slipping and nose-diving that ensued Bob got his big triplane headed for home and started off at high speed. This left the four hunters to their own devices, with no other troubles than to down such German antagonists as they might encounter, and to get their own machines safely home if they could.

But none of the four liked to start for home until he was sure the others of his group were all right and ready to come back with him. The spotty clouds were responsible for a bit of delay. Parker was nowhere to be seen. Joe, Harry, and Jimmy circled round once or twice, undecided what to do, and at that moment Parker came climbing back from a dead-leaf drop, having shaken off his Boche pursuers, and gave the signal for the home flight. Home they turned, and as they did so, four big Albatrosses, a section of the first group they had met, joined to two of the second group, came at them. Without any concerted idea of action Joe, Jimmy, and Harry looped straight over simultaneously, every one of the three performing a perfect loop and coming right side up at the same moment. Each of them, also, fired a round at the Boche immediately in front of him and made off for home at top speed.

Parker did a side-wing drop, and as he did so felt a sharp pain in his back. His arms lost their power. A bullet had lodged in his back, and worked its way, urged, perhaps, by the pressure of the boy's back against the seat cushion, to some spot more vital than that in which it had first lodged. From an apparently harmless wound, and certainly a painless one, Parker's hurt had become so serious as to prove mortal. For, try as he would, he could not move his arms to right his machine. Down he dropped, mercifully losing consciousness as his machine shot toward the earth, and crashing, at last, so fiercely into the ground that naught remained of his hunter and its gallant pilot but a twisted mass of wreckage and a still form maimed out of all recognition. Parker had paid the great price, after a gallant fight.

The other three hunters carried their pilots safely home, able to report that Joe and Jimmy had each accounted for one of the four Albatrosses that had last attacked them.

Three days later their squadron was moved back, and its place taken by a fresh unit. Jimmy Hill was sent to hospital with his slit cheek, but was soon out and about again.

Less than a fortnight later all five of the boys, Joe, Bob, Jimmy, Harry, and Dicky, were on leave in London. The night after their arrival on the English side of the Channel, Archie Fox, now a convalescent, invited them to dinner at the Royal Overseas Officers Club, where the six Brighton boys foregathered merrily.

Dinner over, Joe proposed a toast of "the folks at home." The boys drank it silently. Then Bob Haines rose and raised his glass.

"Let us drink to the luck of the Brighton lot," he said. "May it never entirely desert us."

As they rose and raised their glasses Dicky Mann added: "May we always be ready to give that luck a fighting chance."

Six strong right hands reached forth to grasp another of the six. Six pairs of bright eyes flashed as each caught an answering flash somewhere round the circle. Six hearts beat with the same stout determination as Joe Little voiced their united sentiments when he said in a low tone, "Amen to that. We will."

THE END